ZOO SCHOOL

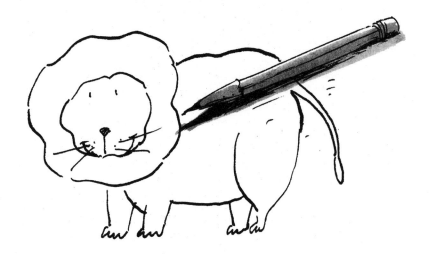

by LAURIE MILLER HORNIK

Illustrated by DEBBIE TILLEY

Clarion Books * New York

Clarion Books
a Houghton Mifflin Company imprint
215 Park Avenue South, New York, NY 10003
Text copyright © 2004 by Laurie Miller Hornik
Illustrations copyright © 2004 by Debbie Tilley

The illustrations were executed in pen and ink.
The text was set in 14-point Centaur.

www.houghtonmifflinbooks.com

Printed in the U.S.A.

Library of Congress Cataloging-in-Publication Data

Hornik, Laurie Miller.
Zoo School / by Laurie Miller Hornik ; illustrated by Debbie Tilley.
      p. cm.
Summary: The students at the strange new Zoo School have never
seen a school like it before, but when inspectors try to close it down
because of irregularities, the students are surprised to find out how
much they have learned.
ISBN 0-618-34204-4
[1. Animals—Fiction. 2. Zoos—Fiction. 3. Schools—Fiction.
4. Humorous stories.] I. Tilley, Debbie, ill. II. Title.
PZ7.H786Zo 2004
[Fic]—dc22   2003018621

QUM 10 9 8 7 6 5 4 3 2 1

For my zooey family:
Rob, Ezra, and Naomi
And for my zooey kindergarten students, 1998–2003
—L. M. H.

For Gillian
—D. T.

Contents

Welcome to the Zoo School,

a new school for children. Which tiger has more stripes than any other? What should you feed a hungry flamingo? Learn these facts and more, all in a zooey setting. Our motto is "Let the Animals Be Your Textbooks!"

For more information, contact
Ms. Font, Principal
555-6100

Tasty Treats Animal Food Supplier

Serving pets and zoo animals everything from canned meats that smell funny to freeze-dried insects with hairy legs. We provide the foods you want your pets to have but are too grossed out to prepare yourself. E-mail us at toogrosstomake@home.com

Squirrel Accidents on the Rise

An alarming increase in the number of squirrel accidents at the zoo has squirrel rights activists up in arms. It seems zoo visitors aren't noticing squirrels on the paths, resulting in injuries to limbs and tails—and sometimes worse. Visitors to the zoo are urged to be cautious. Ms. Hummingfly, zookeeper and squirrel expert, had these words of advice: "Just think WOFS—it stands for Watch Out for Squirrels." Ms. Font, head of the zoo and principal of the Zoo School, was not available for comment.

—by Bea Careful ■

Zoolinda Gray, Chief Zookeeper and Founder of the Zoo School, Dies at the Age of 101

The whole zoo world was saddened last month by the news that Zoolinda Gray had died. "Zoolinda was a wonderful zookeeper. She kept this zoo running tiptop!" said Ms. Hummingfly, a longtime keeper at the zoo.

Mr. Dapple, another zookeeper, said, "Zoolinda had 73 wonderful qualities. I would happily list them all for you right now, but I am 26 minutes late feeding the tigers."

The zoo and the Zoo School are now under the direction of Ms. Font, who was, unfortunately, unavailable for comment.

1

Something Fishy

On the first day of school, Ursula found herself in a sunny classroom right between the Elephant Yard and the Seal Pool. A classroom? Were they kidding? There weren't even any desks—not real desks, anyway. Instead, each chair was behind a desk-shaped fish tank filled with tropical fish. Ursula chose the one with the bright yellow fish and hung her backpack on the chair. She looked around, shaking her head.

Against one wall were huge bags of birdseed and cartons of kibble. There were cans of dog chow, cat chow, and something called turtle chow. There were barrels of peanuts, bales of hay, boxes of fish flakes, and a package of freeze-dried crickets. Gross! On another wall was a classroom job chart and, above it, a banner with the school motto written in large, uneven handwriting: LET THE ANIMALS BE YOUR TEXTBOOKS! There was a strange smell in the classroom, too. It seemed like a combination of peanuts, elephant poop, and rotten bananas.

Ursula couldn't believe her parents were making her go to this ridiculous Zoo School. One minute they see an ad in some magazine (called *Zooey!*, of all things), and the next thing you know, they're yanking her from a perfectly good, perfectly ordinary school and making her go to some silly school in a zoo because it sounds "interesting" and like "the chance of a lifetime." Ursula rolled her eyes. Really!

A mouse skittered across the floor, and the teacher hardly noticed. No, even worse! She seemed to notice but not care. She was busy arranging boxes of fish flakes. She didn't even look like a teacher. She wore tan pants and a tan shirt, with a picture of an elephant sewn on the front pocket. Some little brown pellets were spilling out of her back pockets. And there was something brown smeared on her shoe. Yuck!

On the other side of the room, Kitty smiled as she listened to the seals barking and an elephant trumpeting in the nearby Elephant Yard. She breathed in deeply, smelling that wonderful elephant smell. African. Healthy. Probably female. Kitty knew a lot about animals.

But Kitty was getting impatient. While it was interesting to have a desk filled with fish (7 half-moon angelfish and 3 neon dottybacks), it wasn't that different from her aquarium at home. Kitty already knew which tiger has the most stripes (the Sumatran), and she knew what to feed a hungry

flamingo (shrimp). But there was so much more to learn! How many taste buds does a boa constrictor have? How often should you bathe a gorilla? Kitty wanted to learn every single fact about animals. The Zoo School would be the perfect place to do it—if they would ever get started.

Leo watched the fish inside his desk for a few minutes, but it made him sleepy and he began to doze off. It wasn't all that different from the effect regular desks had on him. They often made him doze off as well. That's why the ad for the Zoo School had caught his eye. After all, how much work could it possibly be to go to school in a zoo? He wondered when it would be time for lunch. There was a peanuty smell in the classroom, and it was making him hungry.

Drake sat at his desk, shaking. He was dreadfully afraid of fish—the way they never shut their eyes and stared at you all the time. It was so creepy! His parents loved fish. And dogs and cats and antelopes and elephants and leopards. In fact, there was no animal his parents didn't love. That's why they had sent Drake to the Zoo School. But they had made a terrible mistake. Drake's parents might find all animals lovable, but Drake found them all terrifying!

Robin had a stomachache. She thought some ginger ale and crackers would be just the thing, but all she could see around the room were weird animal foods. Just thinking about turtle chow made her stomachache worse! What she needed was a trip to the school nurse. At her old school, she sometimes spent half the day in the nurse's office. Cough drops! Band-Aids! Crackers! No matter what was bothering her—a sore throat, a scratch, a stomachache, a boring math lesson, a hard spelling quiz, the first day of school—the nurse always made her feel better, at least for a little while. She would just wait until she could get that teacher's attention. Then she would ask to go to the nurse.

The bell rang. Ursula sighed with relief. A bell! Just like her old school. The children quieted down, and the teacher put away the last box of fish flakes and came over to her desk, brushing little brown pellets off her pants.

"Good morning, class," she said. "I am Ms. Hummingfly, one of the zookeepers here at the zoo. I will also be your teacher."

"You're a zookeeper?" said Leo. "You mean you're not a real teacher?" He wasn't sure if that was a good thing or a bad thing. On the one hand, zookeepers probably didn't know about giving homework. On the other hand, Leo had spent years learning how to get by teachers without having to do too much work. Would it be the same with zookeepers? And would they know when it was time for lunch?

Ms. Hummingfly smiled. "There are two zookeepers here at the zoo—Mr. Dapple and myself—and we are your two teachers as well. The Zoo School is quite small, since it's brand-new. But don't worry! If we can take care of animals, we can take care of children. As Ms. Font always says, 'Animals and people are not that different after all.'"

"Who's Ms. Font?" asked Ursula.

"Our beloved principal, of course. And the founder of the Zoo School. But she's very busy. You won't see her much."

Robin raised her hand. "Ms. Hummingfly, may I please go to the nurse?" she asked. "I have a stomachache."

"Oh, there is no school nurse," said Ms. Hummingfly. "Just us zookeepers. Would you like me to get you something for your stomachache?"

Robin looked again at the shelves of kibble, turtle chow, and freeze-dried crickets. "Uh, that's okay," she said. "It's feeling a little better." She wondered how she would ever get through a whole year at school without a nurse.

Ms. Hummingfly felt badly for this girl who seemed so ill. A few of the other students looked quite out of sorts as well. Ms. Hummingfly wished she knew more about children. If the monkeys were feeling a bit under the weather, she would know just what to give them (bananas, skins removed). If the lizards were sluggish, she had just the thing (crickets and mealworms, extra wiggly). But children—that was a new kind of animal for her. Ms. Hummingfly sighed. She had promised Ms. Font that she would try, and so try she would. She smiled warmly at the sixteen kits, er . . . pups, er . . . children and moved right along with the daily plan.

2
classroom Jobs

Ms. Hummingfly pointed at a large chart on the wall. "Let's get started with our classroom jobs," she said cheerfully.

Drake looked at the chart with relief. He was glad to be looking at anything that wasn't an animal.

"I know what that is!" said Ursula. "That's a job chart. We had one at my old school. All our names are posted with hooks under them. Whatever job is hanging on your hook is your job for the day."

The children ran over to look at the chart.

"I can't tell what the jobs are," said Kitty. "The names of the jobs aren't here—just their initials. Mine is SCG."

"That stands for Squirrel Crossing Guard," said Ms. Hummingfly. "It's up to you to make sure that the squirrels around the zoo cross all the zoo paths safely. That's a very important job." Kitty was surprised. She knew a lot about squirrels (height, weight, speed, eye color, favorite food), but she'd never thought about helping them cross the road safely before.

"I'm LL," said Drake.

"That's Line Leader," said Ms. Hummingfly.

"Oh, we had Line Leader at my old school," said Ursula. "The Line Leader gets to walk in the front of the line and get everywhere first."

Drake gulped. The only place he wanted to get first was out of this scary zoo!

"What's SH?" asked Ursula, reading her job tag. She held her breath and hoped it wasn't Snake Handler, Spider Holder, or anything that had to do with scorpions!

"SH is Snack Helper," said Ms. Hummingfly.

"Yes!" shouted Ursula happily. "A nice, *regular* job!"

"In fact, you can start now," said Ms. Hummingfly. She handed Ursula a box of fish flakes.

"This is our snack?" Ursula asked, dumbfounded.

Ms. Hummingfly chuckled. "Oh, no. It's not *your* snack!" She pointed to the fish swimming inside the desks. "It's *their* snack!" The fish did look kind of hungry.

Ursula shook her head. "Ms. Hummingfly, I was Snack Helper at my old school," she said. "The Snack Helper is in charge of pouring juice and counting out crackers for the other kids. As Snack Helper, I *never* fed fish."

JOB CHA

Drake   Ursula
LL   SH

Leo   Joseph
CH

Kitty   Robir
SCG

"How awful!" said Ms. Hummingfly. "Your fish must not have lasted very long."

Disgusted, Ursula took the box of fish flakes and began sprinkling a few in each desk.

"What's CH?" asked Leo, reading his job tag.

"Cleanup Helper," said Ms. Hummingfly.

Leo sighed. Cleanup Helper sounded like a lot of work. He wished he was Snack Helper instead. Leo loved to eat. Even the fish flakes smelled kind of tasty.

Ms. Hummingfly handed him a broom. Tired already, Leo followed Ursula around and cleaned up the fish flakes she dropped. He tasted a couple, and they weren't that bad, just a bit dry.

Kitty was examining the chart more carefully when she noticed a hook labeled JOSEPH with no job hanging on it.

"Why doesn't Joseph have a job?" she said.

"Oh, Joseph's not here yet," explained Ms. Hummingfly. "Ms. Font said he'd be arriving later in the year. He's coming from very far away."

"Where?" asked Drake, happy to be thinking about people instead of animals.

"I don't remember exactly, but I think it started with an *A*."

"Antarctica?" asked Robin. Ms. Hummingfly shook her head.

"Arizona?" asked Drake. Ms. Hummingfly shook her head again.

Ursula had found a page in her dictionary that listed places that started with the letter *A*.

"Afghanistan. Alabama. Alaska. Albania. Algeria. Andorra. Angola. Antigua. Argentin—"

Ms. Hummingfly sighed. "None of those sound right," she said. "Now, we really should get started. I'm trying to decide if we should read *Goldilocks and the Three Bears* to the bears—they do love the ending—or write poems about how it feels to be a hippopotamus. Hippos have such HUGE feelings—perfect for a poem. What do you think?"

The children stared at her, not knowing what to say.

Just then the bell rang, and Ms. Hummingfly leaped up.

"Oh, dear!" she said. "I never could keep track of time, and I don't want to be late feeding the bears. Go ahead and help yourselves to snack. Mr. Dapple will be here soon for math class."

When Ms. Hummingfly was gone, Ursula slammed her notebook down on her desk. The bright yellow fish (which Kitty knew were long-nose butterfly fish) jiggled around nervously for a moment, then swam on as if nothing had happened.

"This school is ridiculous!" said Ursula.

"I think so, too," said Kitty. "I had hoped to learn facts about animals. You can't learn facts from stories or poems."

"Didn't she say something about snack?" asked Leo. "I'm starving."

"Don't talk about food," said Robin. "My stomach is killing me. What kind of school has no nurse, anyway?"

Drake didn't say anything. One of the fish in his desk had given him the evil eye and he was frozen with fear.

Ursula walked over to the shelves. "I happen to be a very ex-perienced Snack Helper. I can count crackers and pour juice practically with my eyes closed." She pulled out the different boxes and bags. "Giraffe pellets . . . birdseed . . . freeze-dried crickets . . . Hey! There aren't any crackers."

"Giraffe pellets might be okay," said Drake. "Just as long as we avoid the crickets."

"Ew!" cried the others.

"Forget crackers!" said Leo. "Let's get ice cream from the cart. We are in a zoo, after all."

"I don't know," said Ursula. "That's not a regular school snack."

"Look," said Leo. "I don't know if you've noticed, but this place is not a regular school."

Ursula had indeed noticed. She sighed and began counting how many wanted chocolate and how many wanted vanilla so she could get them from the cart. It was much more work than being Snack Helper at her old school but also more delicious.

As the children sat slurping their ice cream, they got very quiet. The only noise was the distant call of the Australian kookaburra bird and a few buzzing bees. Some people think that children are quiet when they eat ice cream because they love it so much. The truth, however, is that it's very good for the brain, and as the children ate their ice cream, they became deep in thought.

I wonder what my class at my old school is studying now, thought Ursula.

How long will it take me to learn every fact about every animal? wondered Kitty.

I hope tomorrow we can learn to make balloon animals, thought

Drake. Drake wasn't scared of balloon animals or, in fact, any kind of balloon.

Do giraffes ever get sore throats? wondered Robin.

Mmmmmmmmmmmmm, thought Leo. He had finished his ice cream and fallen asleep and was already dreaming of the peanut-butter-and-baloney sandwich he had brought for lunch.

3
Everybody counts

When the bell rang and the next zookeeper walked in, the children quieted down, more out of curiosity than respect.

He looked like a giraffe. He wasn't a giraffe, of course. But if you were to try to make a man look like a giraffe, this is what you'd get. He was very tall, with a surprisingly long neck and large goofy eyes. His legs seemed too long for his body. And he was wearing a spotted tie. Upon meeting the gaze of the surprised students, he immediately dropped all of his papers. When he bent down to pick them up, he didn't look so much like a giraffe anymore. He looked like an ostrich burying his head in the sand.

"Good morning, 16 children," he finally said. "Why, what a lovely number 16 is! The square of 4, the square root

of 256, the double of 8. A beautiful number indeed!" He giggled.

The 32 eyes of the 16 children stared at him.

"Welcome to the Zoo School!" he said. "I am Mr. Dapple. I'm a zookeeper here at the zoo, but for 2 hours a day, I'll be your math teacher. Since there are 181 school days, that makes 362 glorious hours of math this year!" He smiled widely. 16 horrified mouths dropped open, revealing 312 teeth.

"What animals do you take care of?" asked Robin, trying to change the subject. All this talk of numbers was giving her a headache on top of her stomachache.

"All different kinds. You see, I am an MZ."

"A what?" asked Drake, hoping it didn't have to do with monkeys or zebras.

"A Mathematical Zoologist. I am in charge of measuring the animals, and weighing their food, and, of course, counting them. I love animals almost as much as I love numbers!" He looked at his watch.

"Speaking of numbers, 4½ minutes have already flown by. We better get started! Your first math assignment is to count how many animals there are in the zoo. You can spend the next 93½ minutes on it. Then we'll meet back here for the last 22 minutes of class to discuss the answer. And it will give all 16 of you a chance to get to know this wonderful zoo. Meanwhile, I need to go take the temperature of the giraffe. It was a little high last night."

* * *

16

Most of the children ran outside, pencils and notebooks in hand, spirits soaring. This school might be weird, but at least here they were, on a school day, outside exploring the zoo!

Only five students lingered on the classroom steps.

"I don't see how counting animals will teach us more about them," said Kitty. "Counting their back molars, maybe, or the ring markings on their tails. But just counting them? I don't get it."

"Please don't talk about animals," said Drake. "They're so scary!"

"You're scared of animals?" Kitty laughed. "Well, why on earth are you at the Zoo School?" Drake didn't answer. He had been wondering the same thing all day.

Kitty was much more interested in animals than in people, but she felt bad for this boy. "Look, don't worry. You can come with me," she said. "Hey, did you know that a giraffe's tongue can be 21 inches long?"

Drake wasn't sure he wanted to know that, but he was relieved not to be facing the animals alone. They headed up the east path toward the flamingos, stopping along the way for Kitty to help a squirrel cross the road safely. She was SCG (Squirrel Crossing Guard) for the day, after all.

Ursula thought counting animals was ridiculous. Math problems were supposed to be in textbooks or on work sheets. *If there are 438 giraffes and 267 leopards, how many animals are there in all?* That was the sort of problem she could understand. Ursula sighed. She tried to look on the bright side. At least this assignment didn't involve reading to bears or writing poems about hippos. She checked her backpack. Pencil, notebook, calculator, dictionary. Yup, she had everything. She headed up the north path toward the bears. She passed the principal's office and, attached to the back of it, the Elephant Yard. Ursula wrote elephants neatly on the left-hand side of her paper, checking the spelling in her dictionary. She counted the elephants. There was one. She wrote 1 neatly next to the word elephants and went to count the lizards.

The sun was shining and a late summer breeze rustled the leaves. Robin's nose was starting to get sunburned. And she felt a slight chill coming on, too. She ran after Ursula to see if she had any suntan lotion in that enormous backpack of hers.

Leo was getting that feeling he'd had so often at his old school. He was simply too tired to do the assignment. Instead, he lay down under a tree outside the classroom and watched the clouds drift lazily across the sky. A group of kids on a field trip walked by, and Leo smiled to himself. *Poor things*, he thought. *They have to go back to regular schools and sit at desks and take tests while I get to lie under a tree, probably all year.* Leo dozed off and had happy peanut-butter dreams.

If Leo hadn't been sleeping quite so soundly, he might have noticed three people with white coats and funny little hats with L.I.O.N.S. written on them. L.I.O.N.S. had nothing to do with the sort of lions you would expect to find at a zoo. It stood for Learned Inspectors of New Schools, and it was their job to inspect each and every new school. L.I.O.N.S. carried thick notebooks filled with questions, and they were already hard at work checking off the answers:

Question 15

Are the students deep in thought? ❏ yes ❏ no

Inspector #1 looked carefully at Leo, who was certainly deep in something. She checked off the little box next to the word *yes.* Inspecting schools was the perfect job for Inspector #1. She came from a long line of inspectors. Her father, Inspector #87, inspected cars (left-front headlights, to be exact). Her mother, Inspector #78, inspected underwear (she was an expert in stretchiness). And it was said that long ago her great-great-great-great-great-great-grandfather, Inspector #1 (after whom she was named), had inspected the pyramids of Egypt.

Question 16

Are the pencils nicely sharpened? ❏ yes ❏ no

Yes. Inspector #2 could tell, even from a distance, that Leo's pencil had a very sharp point indeed. (This wasn't too surprising, since he hadn't used it.) In fact, Inspector #2 had very poor eyesight. He could see only small things and not big things. Inspecting schools was the perfect job for him, since it was generally the little things he was expected to look at—pencil points, tucked-in shirts, neat handwriting, and the small print in his inspector notebook.

Is the math sufficiently challenging? ❏ yes ❏ no

The children were heading back now toward the classroom, and Inspector #3 heard one of them say, "417." She checked off *yes*. Inspector #3 knew a lot about schools. After all, when she was a child, she had gone to one for several years. Inspecting schools was the perfect job for her.

Question 18

Is the principal neatly dressed? ❏ yes ❏ no

This was only the first of many, many, many questions about the principal. They would have to meet with Ms. Font in person to answer these questions. The three inspectors headed over to the principal's office to set up a meeting.

The sound of the children tramping back into the classroom woke Leo. He overheard somebody say, "417." He wrote it on his paper and followed the class inside.

As the children entered the room, Mr. Dapple had them write their answers on the blackboard:

417 417 418 417 416 417 417 417

357 417 417 418 417 415 416 417

Mr. Dapple smiled. He loved being surrounded by numbers. Of course, Mr. Dapple knew there was only one right answer. That was part of what he loved about numbers. And it was his job to help the children find that one answer!

"Would anyone like to explain how they got their answer?" he asked.

Ursula raised her hand. Finally! Regular school with math problems and solutions. Perfect.

"Yes, girl in the 2nd row, 3rd from the left," said Mr. Dapple.

"My name is Ursula."

"Ah, what a nice name. It has 6 letters, with the 1st and 4th being identical. Lovely indeed."

"Yes, well . . . ," said Ursula, and she read off her list:

1	elephant
60	bats
24	squids
2	tigers
9	butterflies
6	flamingos
15	bears
2	lions
3	hippos
1	zebra
2	giraffes
7	gazelles
35	monkeys
5	gorillas

26	snakes
39	frogs
13	lizards
16	turtles
33	birds
3	seals
12	mice
17	hamsters
8	yellow-footed marsupial mice
10	moles
4	possums
2	skunks
2	otters
1	ferret
59	fish

"Yes, that does add up to 417."

"Yay!" cried the other kids who had also gotten 417. Robin, who had gotten 416, looked for her mistake. "I counted only 2 seals," she realized. "The sun was in my eyes." Drake had been too scared to count the bats, so he got only 357.

"But, young lady with the 14 freckles," Mr. Dapple said to Ursula. "What about the other animals in the zoo?"

"There aren't any other animals in the zoo," Ursula said. She might not know much about animals and silly schools in zoos, but Ursula knew about regular school things like counting.

"Ow!" cried Robin. "A mosquito bit me!" The other children ran over to look. Sure enough, a small red bump was just starting to appear on her arm. Robin tried to be brave. It didn't itch yet, but she knew it would start any minute.

"What about that mosquito, for instance?" asked Mr. Dapple.

"Oh," said Ursula. "I guess I didn't think to count it." She wrote 1 mosquito on her list and crossed out 417 and wrote 418.

"And what about the 14 mosquitoes in his family—his mother, father, brother, sister, aunt, and 9 cousins?"

Ursula's mouth hung open, but Mr. Dapple was on a roll now.

"And the 4,875 ants, the 342 fleas, and the 98 pigeons."

"Mr. Dapple, we didn't know you wanted us to count those animals, too," said Robin, trying not to scratch her bite.

But Mr. Dapple was still going. ". . . the 167 squirrels, 49 bees, 11 ladybugs, 16 students, 2 zookeepers, and, of course, our beloved principal, Ms. Font."

"That's not fair," said Drake. "You counted us. We're people, not animals!"

"Human beings are a kind of animal," said Mr. Dapple.

Drake smiled. He had never thought about that. At least there was one animal he wasn't scared of. But then a clown fish swam across his desk and he shuddered.

"What about Joseph, the new student?" asked Leo.

"I don't think we should count him. After all, he's not here yet," said Kitty.

"True," said Mr. Dapple. "We'll add him in when he gets here. Right now, altogether . . ." Mr. Dapple looked at the ceiling for a minute as he figured out the total. "Altogether, 258,762 animals!" Triumphantly, he wrote 258,762 on the blackboard. "As Ms. Font always says, 'Everybody counts!'"

4
A Visit to the Equator

Leo smiled as he unpacked his lunch under a tree outside. A peanut-butter-and-baloney sandwich, a peanut-butter milk shake, and peanut-butter cookies for dessert. Leo firmly believed that peanut butter made everything taste better. He sighed with happiness as he chewed his first bite.

Even Robin was feeling a bit better. Her parents had packed a thermos of chicken soup, some plain crackers, and a few cough drops. She felt that she could make it to the end of the day, if just barely.

Kitty ate her sandwich quickly so that she could get to her favorite part of her lunch—animal crackers. She closed her eyes, pulled an animal cracker out of the box, and took a bite. It had a very strong taste, a bit furry and with a hint of stripes. Kitty smiled. *Tiger,* she thought, then opened her eyes and checked. It was indeed a tiger. The next one tasted wise but rather dry and very filling. *Elephant,* Kitty thought. When you knew as much about animals as Kitty did, you could tell animal crackers apart just by their tastes.

Ursula ate her peanut-butter-and-jelly sandwich without giving it much thought. She didn't even bother eating the animal crackers her mother had sent along in honor of the Zoo School. Ursula wasn't thinking about her lunch. She was thinking about the rest of the day. At her old school, she would know just what to expect this afternoon. Regular classes with regular teachers. Sitting at her desk. Getting homework. The only animal around would be a boring class pet, like a guinea pig, that slept all the time anyway. How Ursula wished for a boring class guinea pig!

Drake ate lunch by himself far from the other children. Both Kitty *and* Ursula had animal crackers in their lunch. As if there weren't enough animals around here already! He could hardly look.

When the bell rang, the children headed back to their classroom. Ms. Hummingfly was waiting for them.

"This afternoon we are going to visit the Equator," she announced.

"Isn't that very far away?" asked Kitty.

Drake was excited. "Field trip!" he cried, delighted at the idea of getting out of the zoo.

26

"It's not so far away. And it's not exactly a field trip," explained Ms. Hummingfly. "The Equator lives on the other side of the Elephant Yard, near the tigers. Haven't you noticed him?"

Ursula shook her head. "Ms. Hummingfly, I learned about the Equator in my old school. A REGULAR school. The Equator is an invisible line that runs around the world. It's not a HIM. It's an IT."

Ms. Hummingfly giggled merrily. Children made the silliest mistakes sometimes. She explained. "The Equator is an invisible LION that runs around the world. Well, that *ran* around the world, anyway. He's quite old now. Oh, and don't mention the invisible part to him. He's sensitive about that. Now, who is LL today?" She checked the chart. "Drake, you are our Line Leader. Everyone line up behind Drake."

Drake sighed. He knew being Line Leader would not be a good thing.

Drake led the way very, very, verrrrrrry slowly toward the lion. He was in no rush to get there. But just as he had always found, he did get there anyway. He shut his eyes tight so he wouldn't have to see the lion. He needn't have bothered. The others were searching all over the Equator's cage, and they couldn't see the lion, either. The cage seemed to be empty.

"Ms. Hummingfly, I can't see him," Leo whispered, so as not to insult the Equator.

"That's because there's NOTHING IN THERE!" cried Ursula, not worried about insulting something that clearly WASN'T THERE.

Ms. Hummingfly gave Ursula a concerned look. This was a student who might need some special attention.

"The Equator deserves our respect," explained Ms. Hummingfly. "He's lived a very full life. In his youth he ran through Brazil, Ecuador, Africa, and Asia. He swam through three oceans. And all that in the blistering heat. He lived in the hottest part of the world."

Ms. Hummingfly was handing out sketchpads and pencils. "Now, let's all do some sketching. Sketching is an excellent way to learn about animals. As Ms. Font always says, 'If you really want to learn about something, you need to see it for yourself.'"

"What's Ms. Font like?" asked Ursula.

"Oh, I've never met her myself, but I hear that she's a firm believer in learning by looking at what's around you."

The children looked around them. Then at the empty cage. And finally at each other.

How do you sketch something that you can't see? wondered Drake.

How do you sketch something that isn't there? wondered Kitty.

How can a school be so ridiculous? wondered Ursula.

I hope I don't get a paper cut, thought Robin. The edge of the paper looked especially sharp.

Kitty knew a lot about animals. She closed her eyes and pictured a lion. Four legs, tail, mane, claws. She shaded under the belly for shadows. Leo copied off of Kitty's picture. He figured it wasn't cheating. Sketching meant drawing what you could see, and what Leo could see was Kitty's drawing of a lion.

Ursula just stared at the cage and dreamed about her old school. They had always sketched things they could see. It might have been boring, but it was also sensible.

The children were so busy studying the Equator that they didn't notice they were being studied as well. Across the path stood the three inspectors, with their notebooks.

Question 134

Do the students use notebooks and pads to record their work? ❑ yes ❑ no

Yes. Inspector #2 couldn't see the lion itself, but he could see the pads in which the children were drawing pictures of the lion.

Question 135

Do the students concentrate hard on their work? ❑ yes ❑ no

Yes. It was true. The children were all concentrating so hard that none of them even saw the inspectors.

The inspectors had seen enough for today. They closed their notebooks and headed toward Ms. Font's office. Ms. Font had been unavailable earlier. The inspectors still needed to schedule an appointment and arrange to drop off some tests that were part of their inspection as well.

"All right, children," said Ms. Hummingfly. "Please bring me your sketchpads and line up. It's time we let the Equator rest. This has been a busy morning for him."

Ursula slammed her pad shut. She hated not to finish her work, but what was she supposed to do? It wasn't her fault the assignment was so ridiculous. She handed in her pad and lined up with the others.

Back at the classroom, Ms. Hummingfly held the drawings up one by one. She admired Drake's sketch, even though it looked more like a housecat than a lion. Leo's was a bit better, but he had forgotten to draw the tail. Kitty's picture was far better. Her lion looked like a real lion, very majestic and almost three-dimensional. Everyone oohed and aahed. Lastly, Ms. Hummingfly held up Ursula's pad. The page was empty.

"Oh!" Ms. Hummingfly cried. Ursula could feel her cheeks getting hot. She opened her mouth to try to explain, but Ms. Hummingfly interrupted. "Ursula, you've really captured him in your sketch. Even his invisibility. How marvelous!" Ms. Hummingfly beamed at Ursula. Perhaps she had been too quick to be so concerned. Ursula might turn out to be an excellent student after all.

5

Hippoppoppopopopotamus

That night, Drake had nightmares filled with tropical fish. But by morning he had a plan. The good thing about fish, he realized, is that they are very quiet and if you didn't look at them, you would hardly know they are there. So the next day he arrived at school with a blanket to cover his desk.

He walked with new confidence into the room, ready to face his day—and the fish. The classroom seemed much noisier. He stared in horror. The fish were gone from the desks. Instead, each desk was filled with a complicated system of see-through tunnels and exercise wheels. Hamsters, mice, moles, possums, otters, and ferrets skittered around inside. Something rolled across the floor. It was a mole in an exercise ball. It banged into a possum in a larger exercise ball, which banged into Joseph's empty chair. The classroom looked like an amusement park ball pit gone crazy!

"Where are the fish?" Drake cried in dismay, almost missing them. He wished he was Joseph. Then he wouldn't be here, either.

"The fish?" said Ms. Hummingfly. "Oh, yes, I quite like them, too. But they had to go back to the aquarium. We use the desks at the Zoo School for animal overflow, you see. We keep animals here while we're cleaning out their habitats. Don't worry! You've got all sorts of small mammals to keep you company today."

"There are so many!" cried Drake.

Ms. Hummingfly said, "As Ms. Font always says, 'If a little of a good thing is good, then a lot of a good thing is even better.'"

Drake shuddered and put his blanket over his head instead of his desk, but he could still hear the squeaking.

"What wonderful rodents!" cried Kitty.

"Mice, hamsters, and moles *are* rodents," agreed Ms. Hummingfly. "But ferrets and otters are mustelids—that means they are in the weasel family. And possums and yellow-footed marsupial mice are marsupials."

"Oh, I didn't see them," said Kitty. "Of course!"

"What's a marsupial?" asked Robin, feeling a bit itchy. She wondered if she was allergic to marsupials, whatever they were.

"It's an animal that grows in its mother's pouch, like a kangaroo," said Kitty.

"But we don't have any kangaroos at the zoo, unfortunately," said Ms. Hummingfly. "Because the zoo is small, the rodents, the mustelids, and the marsupials live together in the Small Mammals House."

Drake didn't care whether they were rodents or mustelids or marsupials. Whatever they were, these animals were scary. A possum-filled exercise ball was headed right for him! He raised his feet just in time.

"Let's get started with those classroom jobs," said Ms. Hummingfly.

Kitty was SH (Snack Helper), so she began sorting mice food from mole food. She knew it was important that each animal got the right type of food. Leo wished she'd get started taking their ice cream orders for later. He knew it was important that each child got the right flavor of ice cream.

Ursula was CH (Cleanup Helper). Ms. Hummingfly handed her a broom and pointed. There was mouse poop everywhere. Ursula shook her head as she cleaned. *Cracker crumbs! Bits of paper!* she thought. *That's what a Cleanup Helper should be cleaning up at school. They should have called this job PH (Poop Helper)!*

Drake was HG, but he was too afraid to ask what it stood for. He feared it might have to do with hugging gorillas.

Ms. Hummingfly said, "This morning we are going to study the hippopotamus. We can write poems about their feelings. We can have lively discussions about mud. And I have a wonderful book to read you, too." She held up a thick book with *Reflections on a Hippopotamus* inscribed on the cover in gold ink. "But let's start with what *you* want to learn about. Ms. Font always says, 'Children learn the most when they study what they are interested in.'"

Leo yawned and put his head down on his desk. It was just about time for his morning snooze.

SCRITCH SCRATCH.

He bolted upright. He'd never get to sleep with those mice skittering around in there. He smiled and shook his head. The teachers at his old school would have appreciated this trick.

If this was Drake's old school, just upon hearing the word *hippopotamus* he would have hidden under his desk. But as much as he was afraid of the word *hippopotamus*, here at the Zoo School he was even more afraid of his desk!

Kitty waved her hand excitedly. "I know a lot about hippos already," she said. "*Hippopotamus* means 'river horse.' It's the third-largest animal that lives on land. Hippopotami (that's the plural) are related to camels, deer, and pigs. They eat 130 pounds of food a day and can grow to weigh 5,800 pounds!"

Ms. Hummingfly smiled. "You do know a lot about the hippopotamus. That's an excellent start for our morning lesson."

Ursula couldn't stand it. Study hippos all morning? Ridiculous! How could learning about hippos possibly help her in later life? School was for learning important things, like math, handwriting, and spelling. Spelling! That's it! She raised her hand.

"Yes, Ursula?"

"I would like to know how many *p*'s there are in *hippopotamus*."

It wasn't what Ms. Hummingfly had expected, but it was a fair question.

"Okay, let's find out," she said.

Relieved to be doing some ordinary schoolwork, Ursula opened her dictionary.

"Line up, please," said Ms. Hummingfly. Ursula looked up in surprise.

Ms. Hummingfly smiled at her. "Ms. Font always says, 'Children learn best from experience.' You could just look *hippopotamus* up in a dictionary, but you probably wouldn't remember how to spell it. However, if you learn to spell *hippopotamus* while looking at a hippopotamus, then you'll know it forever."

Ursula shook her head. That was the trouble with having zookeepers as teachers. They didn't appreciate the importance of a good dictionary.

"Now, who's our HG?" asked Ms. Hummingfly. Drake raised his hand.

"We need you up front."

"W-w-what's a-a-a HG?" Drake asked in barely a whisper, thinking he'd rather not even know.

"Hippopotamus Greeter, of course," said Ms. Humming-fly. "It will be your job to greet the hippos first." Drake groaned. First LL and now HG. What terrible luck!

Ursula lined up with the others, but she took her dictionary with her. She always did.

Only Robin didn't line up. She had a teeny-tiny little bump on her left thumb. She showed Ms. Hummingfly. "I need a Band-Aid," she said.

"Poor dear!" said Ms. Hummingfly. "Let's get you fixed up."

Ms. Hummingfly reached into her back pocket and pulled out a huge box labeled HIPPO FIRST-AID KIT. She pulled out the largest Band-Aid Robin had ever seen.

"Sorry it's so big," she said. "But it's the kind I use on hippos." She helped Robin put it on. It covered her entire arm up to her elbow. But it also covered the teeny-tiny little bump on her left thumb, so Robin was happy, at least for now.

When the class arrived at the Hippo Pond, Ms. Hummingfly had them wait while Drake greeted the hippos. Shaking, he managed a small hello and a wave of his hand. Then he hid behind a rock to recover.

"Children," said Ms. Hummingfly. "Our question is, 'How many *p*'s are there in *hippopotamus*?' Ms. Font always says to try to solve a problem in *several different ways*." So while Kitty and Robin looked on the plaque that said HIPPOPOTA-MUS and counted the *p*'s, Leo called out to one of the hippos, "Excuse me, how many *p*'s are there in *hippopotamus?*" The hippo looked him square in the eye, or so it seemed to Leo. Then he (the hippo, not Leo) lumbered out of the water and lifted one leg in the air.

"Did you see that?" Leo called to Drake. Drake had not seen it. He was still hiding behind a rock. He was dreadfully afraid of hippos, no matter how you spelled them.

"That hippo just lifted one leg. He must be telling me there's one *p* in *hippopotamus.*"

Drake was a little better at spelling. "I know it's more than one. Maybe he was telling you there are three *p*'s because he *didn't lift* three legs."

Ursula was disgusted. "You can't find out how to *spell* hippopotamus by *asking* a hippopotamus!" Spelling was learned by doing work sheets and looking things up in dictionaries, just like at her old school. Everyone knew that. Ursula was now in the *h*'s in her dictionary—*Hexateuch . . . hidalgo . . . hieroglyph . . . hippodrome.* She was getting close.

Ms. Hummingfly smiled. "Ursula, do you know how to spell *girl?*"

"Of course. *G-i-r-l,*" said Ursula. That was easy. She didn't even need her dictionary.

"Drake, do you know how to spell *boy?*"

"*B-o-y,*" said Drake, smiling. He wasn't afraid of spelling.

"So, if a girl can spell *girl* and a boy can spell *boy,* why couldn't a hippopotamus spell *hippopotamus?*" The children nodded. It made sense, sort of, if you didn't think about it too hard.

"*H! I! P-P-O! P-O-T! A-M-U-S!*" chanted the children as they followed Ms. Hummingfly back to class. This was the most fun spelling lesson any of them could remember. Even Drake found that a hippopotamus wasn't so scary once you knew how to spell it.

Only Ursula wasn't chanting. She lugged her dictionary, disgusted. What a silly school! As she neared the classroom, she saw three people in white coats and funny hats that said L.I.O.N.S. on them. They carried thick notebooks. One of them pointed at Ursula and cried with glee, "*Question 252. Do students use reference books such as dictionaries?* Yes, indeed!" They scribbled quickly in their thick notebooks, and then they were gone.

Ursula wondered what L.I.O.N.S. stood for. She wrote it down so she would remember to ask.

6
Having Butterflies

"What's L.I.O.N.S.?" Ursula asked Mr. Dapple. Everyone had finished his or her snack, except Robin, who found that a second ice cream cone had made both her sore throat *and* her stomachache feel better.

"That's easy," said Leo. "It spells *lions*." He was surprised Ursula didn't know that, since she was so fond of spelling.

"I know it spells *lions*," Ursula said, annoyed. "I want to know who those people are wearing hats with L.I.O.N.S. written on them. One of them seemed very excited about my dictionary. Are they zookeepers?"

"Oh, no," said Mr. Dapple. "They're inspectors. L.I.O.N.S. stands for Learned Inspectors of New Schools. They've come to inspect the Zoo School. In fact, Ms. Font just sent over these L.I.O.N.S. tests. You're supposed to take them today." He pointed to a huge stack of test booklets on his desk. "The test has 300 questions and each question has 7 possible answers!" he said excitedly.

Drake thought the L.I.O.N.S. test sounded almost as scary as real lions.

"Everyone, take out a number 2 pencil," said Mr. Dapple. "Would the Test Booklet Passer please begin to pass out the tests?"

Leo was TBP (Test Booklet Passer). He wished he was PBT (Peanut-Butter Taster) instead. Those test booklets looked awfully heavy. He thought a little lunch first might help.

"But what exactly do the inspectors do?" asked Ursula, getting frustrated. Mr. Dapple wasn't very good at explaining things unless they had numbers in them.

Mr. Dapple thought hard. He knew he wasn't very good at explaining things unless they had numbers in them. He tried again.

"There are 3 L.I.O.N.S. inspectors," he said. "Inspector #1, Inspector #2, and Inspector #3. They are in charge of inspecting every new school. They give tests, visit the school, and interview the principal, of course. Each inspector has a thick notebook with 99 pages in it and 9 questions on each page. That's 891 questions in all! If the school passes the inspection, it gets a gold seal of approval."

"A seal?" cried Drake, looking around anxiously. But then he realized Mr. Dapple didn't mean that kind of seal.

"What if the school *doesn't* pass the inspection?" asked

Ursula. She wasn't sure what L.I.O.N.S. would think of the Zoo School, but she knew what *she* thought of it so far.

"Then the school has to close immediately," Mr. Dapple explained. The children looked at each other. Some of them thought that might not be so bad.

"Now, please take out a number 2 pencil," Mr. Dapple said, for the 2nd time.

"But school just started!" said Kitty. "Shouldn't we take the test at the end of the year instead?"

"Yeah," said Drake. "Joseph isn't even here yet. He won't get to take it."

"They have to give the tests early," explained Mr. Dapple, "or there wouldn't be enough time to grade them. They use special machines to mark them, and it takes 142 days. For the 3rd time, please take out a number 2 pencil. When you get your test booklet, please turn directly to page 3, skipping pages 1 and 2. You will start with question number 1, at the bottom of page—"

Robin interrupted. "Mr. Dapple, I don't feel well." It was true. Robin had a weird feeling all over. She remembered feeling this way when it was time for a test at her old school. She would go to the nurse, and, by the time the rest of the class had finished the test, she always felt much better.

"What's wrong?" asked Mr. Dapple.

"I'm not sure," said Robin.

Mr. Dapple sighed. He was more interested in numbers than in children, but this girl with the 2 pigtails and the 3 Band-Aids really looked unwell.

"Let's see what we can do," said Mr. Dapple. He reached into his front pocket and pulled out a teeny-tiny box labeled INSECT FIRST-AID KIT. Inside were three small white spray bottles.

"We have nectar-flavored antennae cleaner, daisy-spiced wing strengthener, or rotten-fruit-scented human repellent," Mr. Dapple said. "What'll it be?"

Robin frowned. She had hoped for something cherry flavored, but daisies would have to do. "I'll try the wing

strengthener," she said, sticking out her elbows since she didn't have any wings. Mr. Dapple spritzed each elbow twice.

"EW!" cried the other children, running as far away from Robin as possible. Robin wished she could run away from herself, too. She smelled awful.

Mr. Dapple read the bottle again. "Oops, sorry! That was the human repellent. I must have gotten them mixed up."

Robin wiped her elbows vigorously with a tissue, and the smell began to go away.

"Do you want to try again?" asked Mr. Dapple, holding up the other bottles.

Robin sighed. "I guess I'll just take the test," she said. Anything was better than rotten-fruit-scented elbows.

"Tests make me nervous," said Kitty. She knew a lot of facts about animals, but she wasn't sure if that's what would be on the test.

"I have butterflies in my stomach," agreed Drake with a shudder. He was dreadfully afraid of butterflies.

"How many?" asked Mr. Dapple.

"How many what?" asked Drake, worried that the test had already started. He didn't want to get the very first question wrong.

"How many butterflies are in your stomach?"

"I don't know," said Drake. "It doesn't really matter, does it?"

Mr. Dapple looked shocked. "Of course it matters! Let's go to the Butterfly Garden and see if that helps us figure it out."

"But don't we have to take the test?" asked Ursula. She was the only one who wanted to take it. She didn't like tests, either, but at least they were part of *regular* school. You weren't supposed to like them.

"Shh!" said the others. "Don't remind him."

"Well, I know you're supposed to take the test right now, but Ms. Font always says, 'Never put off learning something new!'"

Some of the other children felt better now, since it seemed they wouldn't be taking the test, at least for a while. But Drake was still worried. How would they count the butterflies in his stomach? He remembered the time he had to have his appendix out. He had stayed in the hospital overnight. Would it be like that? As he thought about it, he got even more butterflies in his stomach. He trailed after the line, feeling more and more worried.

At the Butterfly Garden, Mr. Dapple began the tour. Drake hid behind a pole. "There are 19,534 different kinds of butterflies in the world, although we only have 3 kinds at our zoo. Those 6 over there are Milbert's tortoiseshell butterflies. Each one can lay up to 900 eggs!

"These 3 here are sleepy orange butterflies." They were indeed orange, although they didn't look sleepy. Leo yawned. Just hearing the word *sleepy* was making *him* sleepy. "They have a 1½-inch wingspan and they like to eat clover. You know what the lucky ones eat?"

"What?" asked Ursula.

"A 4-leaf clover!" Mr. Dapple chuckled. He loved jokes with numbers in them. The children groaned.

"And over here we have the stomach butterflies," Mr. Dapple continued, pointing to a window filled with little blue butterflies fluttering madly. "They are brand-new at the zoo. They just arrived this morning! See how they're flying around frantically? They're the kind you generally get in your stomach." Drake read the plaque:

STOMACH BUTTERFLIES
**Occurring naturally in the stomachs of
anxious children, they are entirely harmless
and go away by themselves when the cause
of the nervousness disappears.**

"Children," Mr. Dapple said, "stomach butterflies are very hard to count since they flap their wings 213 times per second and fly at a speed of 257 feet per minute. But let's try counting the ones in the window. It's good practice."

All the children tried, except Drake.

"11!" said Leo.

"99!" said Robin.

"37!" said Ursula.

"241!" said Kitty.

Mr. Dapple shook his head. "There are actually 242," he

said. "But good tries, everyone. As I said, they are very hard to count."

Wow, Drake thought, *if there are 242 in that window, I must have at least 300 in my stomach.* He was still worried about the test.

Mr. Dapple looked at his watch. "Only 132 seconds until lunchtime! I guess we won't have time for that test after all. I'll have to return them to Ms. Font as they are. We have just enough time for Drake to tell us how many butterflies are in his stomach."

Drake smiled. Did Mr. Dapple say no test?

"Zero!" he said happily.

"Excellent counting!"

Dear Ms. Font,

Thank you for sending the tests back
so promptly. They will be marked by our
special machines. In the meantime, we will
continue to thoroughly inspect the Zoo
School. We will examine the classroom,
watch lessons, evaluate classroom materials,
and, of course, meet with you.

Please schedule an appointment with us at
your earliest convenience, as the principal
interview is a very important part of the
inspection process.

Sincerely,

Inspector #1, Inspector #2, and Inspector #3
L.I.O.N.S.
(Learned Inspectors of New Schools)

7

Batty

"Hell-o-o-o," Drake called softly as he entered the classroom. It was his turn to be SCG, so he was a few minutes late. The squirrel traffic had been quite heavy.

The classroom lights were off and the shades were drawn. The classroom smelled the same as usual (peanuts, elephant poop, rotten bananas), but it was as black as night. Drake had come to expect the unexpected. After all, he had been going to the Zoo School for several weeks already. But this was unusual even for the Zoo School.

"Come on in," called a voice that sounded like Ms. Hummingfly's.

"Um, that's okay," said Drake. He was dreadfully afraid of the dark.

"You're not afraid of the dark, too, are you?" called a voice that sounded like Ursula's.

"Leave him alone," called a voice that sounded like Kitty's. "It's all right, Drake. The lights are out so that the animals in our desks will feel more comfortable. There's nothing to worry about."

Very slowly, Drake made his way into the classroom. He felt around for his desk and chair and sat down.

"Whew," he said, relieved. "I guess I'm not as afraid of the dark as I thought I was. As long as it's not a cave filled with bats, that is." Drake giggled nervously. His eyes were starting to adjust to the dark. He saw Kitty and Ursula and Robin and Leo and a few other kids. He saw Ms. Hummingfly at the front of the room, riffling through some papers.

"You don't like bats?" asked Leo.

"I hate them."

"Well, you better not look in your desk, then."

Drake looked. "Aaaaaaaaahhhhhhhh!" he cried.

His desk—and all the desks—were filled with dark brown furry bats, all huddled together, pawing frantically and squeaking like mice. Kitty knew they were Mexican free-tailed bats and that they had a wingspan of 12 inches, but she didn't get a chance to tell Drake because just then the lights flicked on.

Drake and the bats all froze in the bright, sudden light.

Three people in white coats stood at the door. They wore L.I.O.N.S. hats and carried notebooks.

"How unusual to start the day in the dark like that," one of them remarked. "I'll have to make a note of it." She scribbled something in her notebook, then stuck out her hand to Ms. Hummingfly.

"Hello, I am Inspector #1, and this is Inspector #2 and Inspector #3. We're here to take a look at the classroom."

"My! What beautiful old wooden desks," said Inspector #2, squinting. "Walnut, isn't it? The wood practically vibrates with age."

Kitty couldn't believe it. "They don't notice the bats! They think the desks are just made of wood the color of bats," she whispered.

"Those inspectors must be really dumb," whispered Ursula.

"Or maybe they aren't looking for bats," Leo said. "So they don't see them."

Drake wished he couldn't see the bats, either.

"They said they're here to look at the classroom, but mostly they're just looking in their notebooks," said Robin.

It was true. Ms. Hummingfly was speaking now, but the inspectors hardly even looked up.

"Well," said Ms. Hummingfly. "We're off. Make sure to turn the lights off when you leave. It makes me *batty* when people leave the lights on." She chuckled.

"Absolutely," said Inspector #1, smiling. She was searching through her notebook for question 769, which she remembered had something to do with conserving energy. Inspector #2 was busy examining the cans of turtle chow along the wall. Inspector #3 sniffed deeply, then wrinkled her nose.

"Where are we going?" asked Leo.

"Gym class," said Ms. Hummingfly.

"Hooray!" yelled the children.

"Is this a good time to ask for a Band-Aid?" Robin asked.

"Can we play basketball today?" Drake asked Ms. Hummingfly. "That's my favorite!"

"Oh, no, not basketball," said Ms. Hummingfly.

"Dodgeball?" asked Ursula.

Ms. Hummingfly shook her head.

"Volleyball?" asked Kitty.

Ms. Hummingfly just shook her head again.

Robin was relieved. She had suffered many gym-related injuries over the years—her finger (a basketball hit it), her nose (a volleyball hit it), her leg (a dodgeball hit it). She hoped that gym at the Zoo School would be more gentle.

"What *will* we play, then?" Robin asked.

"There are many exciting choices, all befitting the Zoo School and all specially designed by Ms. Font herself. We have Running with Gazelles, Wrestling with Lions, Weight-lifting with Gorillas, Diving with Seals, and Monkey Bars—"

"Let me guess," interrupted Ursula. "—with Monkeys?"

"Exactly!" said Ms. Hummingfly. "Ms. Font always says it's important for children to have choices, so what would you all like to do first?"

"Let's do Monkey Bars," said Ursula. "We had them in my old school. Without real monkeys, of course."

"No, let's do Running Away from Gazelles,'" said Drake. He'd been spending a good deal of time in the Zoo School running away from animals already.

"It's not Running AWAY FROM Gazelles," said Kitty.

"It's Running WITH Gazelles. Gazelles can run 50 miles per hour. They're among the fastest land animals, although not as fast as cheetahs."

"I know there are lots of good choices," said Ms. Hummingfly, "but if it takes too long to decide, you won't have time for any of them today. Let's just start with Wrestling with Lions. After all, the lions are just *lion* around anyway." She chuckled.

"Uh, that's okay," said Drake. "We can decide!"

"Yeah! We wouldn't want Joseph to miss out on Wrestling with Lions," said Leo. He was just as scared of wrestling with real lions as Drake was. They all were.

"In my old school, when we couldn't decide about something, we used to do 'Eeny-meeny-miney-mo-catch-a-tiger-by-the-toe,' and whoever it landed on got to pick," said Ursula.

"You can't catch a tiger by the toe," said Kitty. "Tigers are much too big. A male tiger weighs about 420 pounds, you know." The others glared at her. "Oh, fine," she said. "I guess it's okay just to *talk* about catching a tiger by the toe."

They did "Eeny-meeny-miney-mo," and it landed on Robin. "I pick Diving with Seals," she said. The Seal Pool reminded her of a nice warm bath. She had heard that a warm bath was good for sore muscles. She hoped it would help, as she was feeling a bit achy from all this talk about gym class.

8
Gym class

When they got to the Seal Pool, the seals were snoozing on the rocks, soaking up the October sun.

"That's my kind of gym class," said Leo.

"They'll be awake soon enough," said Ms. Hummingfly. "It's almost their feeding time."

Leo's stomach gurgled. He wished it was almost *his* feeding time.

"Seals are excellent divers, you know," said Ms. Hummingfly. "Elephant seals are the best divers of all sea mammals—even better than whales! They can hold their breath underwater for more than twenty minutes."

Drake was taking deep breaths himself to try to stay calm. He couldn't believe he was supposed to get in the water with these animals.

"You can change in those bathrooms," said Ms. Hummingfly, pointing. "Meanwhile, I'll go get the fish."

When they got back to the Seal Pool, Ms. Hummingfly had a big bucket of fish. The seals had woken up and were looking at it with great interest.

"We've trained the seals to do all sorts of tricks. They'll do almost anything for food," said Ms. Hummingfly. "Watch!"

Everyone watched.

"Silver Streak, this one's for you!" Ms. Hummingfly cried. She threw a fish. A shiny seal leaped off the rock, caught the fish in midair, spun around twice, and then dove down deep into the water. He came up a minute later with no sign of the fish. The children all clapped.

"Good job, Silver Streak. Twitcher, you're up." A smaller seal leaped for her fish. She bounced it off the end of her nose, then caught it in her mouth and dove into the green water. She came up, nose twitching, looking proud. The children clapped harder.

This wasn't like gym class at Ursula's old school, but she was so busy clapping that she hardly noticed.

"This one's for Flipsy!" said Ms. Hummingfly, throwing a fish. The third seal did a back flip off the rock. She missed the fish but dove after it into the water. She came up a minute later, licking her lips. The children clapped even harder. These seals were amazing!

Ms. Hummingfly threw more fish to each seal in order until the bucket was empty. The seals swam a few laps around the pool, then climbed back on their rock to rest in the sun.

"Now it's your turn," Ms. Hummingfly told the children. "Kitty, you're up first."

Kitty climbed onto the edge of the pool. She knew a lot about seals. She knew there are two main types of seals—earless seals and eared seals. Both can hear, but the earless seals don't have earflaps, just openings. The earless seals use their back flippers to help them swim like fish. They are better divers than the eared seals. This is what Kitty thought about while she dove.

It didn't really help.

Kitty hit the water with a huge *thwack* and came up sputtering. The children clapped politely. Kitty wondered if her earflaps had gotten in the way.

Robin's dive splashed all the children and Ms. Hummingfly. There were puddles everywhere! Most of the children didn't even bother to clap. Robin's eyes stung a bit from the water, but at least she wasn't as achy anymore.

Drake's turn was next, but he refused to dive at all. It was too scary.

"That's okay," said Ms. Hummingfly. "Why don't you clean up some of these puddles? You wouldn't want any squirrels slipping on them." Drake sighed with relief and went to get the mop.

He got back just in time for Ursula's turn. It was a good thing he did, because her dive was even splashier! No one clapped. They were hardly even bothering to watch anymore. Everyone was hungry and tired of gym class. Drake tried to mop the puddles, but he was so wet from being splashed that he seemed to make new puddles faster than he could mop up the old ones.

"Okay, Leo," said Ms. Hummingfly. "You're the last one. After your dive, we'll have snack. Since you've been working so hard, I got you all ice cream sandwiches!" She held one up for them to see.

Leo was much too tired to dive. But he loved ice cream sandwiches. As he tried to decide what to do, Ms. Hummingfly slipped on a puddle Drake had been trying to mop up.

"Leaping lizards!" she cried. The ice cream sandwich flew out of her hands, right over the water.

"I've got it!" cried Leo. In one fluid motion, he dove off the side of the pool, did three somersaults in the air, and caught the ice cream sandwich in his teeth. He landed noiselessly in the water with hardly even a splash.

"Where did he go?" cried the children. They stared intently into the water. Ms. Hummingfly looked nervous. She started to climb over the side of the pool in case she needed to rescue him.

"I see him!" cried Drake. Sure enough, there was Leo, swimming in a circle around the Seal Pool, slurping up his ice cream sandwich. Finally, after circling the pool three times, he popped his head out of the water and smacked his lips. The ice cream sandwich was gone. The children clapped wildly.

Leo climbed onto the rock and curled up next to a seal.

"Good snack," he murmured as he drifted off to sleep. The other children smiled. Leo would do almost anything for food.

Dear Ms. Font,

What beautiful walnut desks you have. In all our years of inspecting schools, we have come across nothing quite like them.

We were so pleased to see the teacher keeping the lights turned off whenever possible. They were even off while the room was filled with children. We applaud your commitment to conserving energy.

The wall displays of authentic animal food are excellent. It is wonderful to have such items where children can actually touch them for "hands-on" learning.

There is, however, quite an unbearable smell in the classroom. While we commend "hands-on" learning, it does not extend to "noses-on" learning when it comes to awful smells. Please have it taken care of immediately.

Also, may we remind you that we are still waiting to meet with you at your earliest convenience in order to complete the principal interview part of the inspection.

Sincerely,

Inspector #1, Inspector #2, and Inspector #3
L.I.O.N.S.
(Learned Inspectors of New Schools)

9

Blue Flamingos

The next day, when the children arrived at their classroom, there was a big sign on the door, written in uneven handwriting:

SKUNKS IN DESKS TODAY
TO COVER SMELL IN CLASSROOM
GO STRAIGHT TO FLAMINGO
LAKE FOR MATH CLASS

From the outside, the classroom didn't smell any worse than usual, but the children weren't taking any chances. This time, Drake wasn't the only one running away. All the children took off as fast as they could, stopping only to check their jobs, which, as usual, they didn't understand anyway. They headed down the west path, glad to be getting so far away from their classroom. They kept walking but soon came to a place where the path was roped off. There was a large orange sign:

DETOUR ⇨

"That's right," said Kitty. "The Tiger Pen is getting some new trees this week."

"I'm glad they didn't put the tigers in our classroom," said Drake. They followed the signs until they got to a lovely patch of grass. Leo sat down to rest, but Kitty spotted another sign:

⇓ PLEASE KEEP OFF THE GRASS ⇓

Grumbling, Leo stood up. They kept walking, past the Bear Den, past the Rain Forest Room, and past a large pile of peanut shells.

"That's odd," said Kitty, looking at the shells.

"Maybe some squirrels ate them," said Leo.

"That's a lot of peanut shells for a few squirrels," said Kitty.

Just then, the children spotted another sign.

"Oh, no!" they groaned.

"No, this is a good one," said Ursula.

FLAMINGOS THIS WAY ⇨

"Yay!" cried the children, glad they were almost there. They were tired from carrying their lunch boxes and school bags this whole time. Ursula, of course, had been carrying her dictionary as well.

The next sign said:

FLAMINGOS

But they didn't even need to read it, because standing behind the sign were six beautiful pink flamingos.

"Look!" cried Mr. Dapple. He was pointing to the flamingos with great excitement. "Isn't that unbelievable?"

The children weren't sure what he meant.

"They're very pretty," said Ursula.

"They're very scary!" said Drake.

"They're very hungry!" cried Leo. A flamingo had grabbed hold of his hood with its beak and was trying to eat it.

"No, no!" said Mr. Dapple. "Don't you see? One of the flamingos has exactly 600 feathers. Not 599. Not 601. But exactly 600! Your first assignment is to figure out which one." Leo was thinking more about beaks than feathers at the moment, but the others tried to do some counting.

"I think it's this one," said Kitty after a minute, pointing to the flamingo that had attached itself to Leo's jacket. "It's an Andean flamingo," she added. "They are very rare."

"You're right," Mr. Dapple said, beaming.

"I don't care what kind it is or how many feathers it has!" cried Leo. "Just make it let go!"

Mr. Dapple disentangled Leo from the flamingo's beak.

Robin rubbed Leo's neck for him until it felt better.

"Those flamingos sure are hungry," said Mr. Dapple, looking at his watch. "No wonder! Ms. Hummingfly was supposed to feed them 27 minutes ago. She must have lost track of time. I'll just go get their food myself. Why don't you have your snack, too, and I'll meet you back here in approximately 34 minutes."

The nearest cart had salted pretzels and cheese popcorn. The kids sat on a stone wall across from the flamingos, licking their salty, cheesy fingers. Only Leo wasn't eating.

"Poor Andean flamingo," said Leo. "You can have some of my snack." He held his cheese popcorn out to the flamingo. The others stared in amazement. Leo loved to eat. He never shared his snack with anyone.

"Uh-oh, better read the sign," said Drake, pointing.

PLEASE DO NOT FEED THE FLAMINGOS

Leo sighed. "There are too many signs around this zoo. The flamingos are hungry and I have food. Why can't I feed them?"

"I know why," said Robin. "Because flamingos don't eat people food. It might make them sick."

"And they could choke," said Ursula. "Animals mouths and throats are different from ours. They aren't made for people food."

Kitty said, "But there's another reason, too. I read that flamingos get their pink color from their special diet. They eat pink food, such as shrimp. If they don't eat pink food, they lose their color."

"Cool!" said Leo. "If pink food makes them pink, then maybe eating blueberries would make—"

"Blue flamingos!" cried Drake. He thought he might not be as scared of blue flamingos. They sounded more silly than scary.

"I don't think that would work," said Kitty. "I've never heard of a blue flamingo."

"That's just because no one ever thought to try it before," said Drake.

Ursula said, "It reminds me of this experiment we did once in my old *regular* school. We put celery into cups of colored water. When the celery sucked up the water, it turned whatever color the water was."

"I don't think we should," said Kitty.

"Why not?" asked Leo. "They might look cool."

"Well, maybe to us," said Kitty. "But they might be embarrassed in front of the other flamingos. What if you turned bright green? Wouldn't you feel silly? Green wouldn't be the right color for you."

Drake, who turned bright pink whenever he was scared,

thought how glad he was not to turn bright green. Pink was bad enough!

"All this talk about food is making me hungry again," said Robin, who had already finished her snack. She always felt a bit dizzy when she was hungry.

"You can have some of mine," said Leo. He reached for his bag of cheese popcorn.

"Hey! Where'd my popcorn go? It was just here."

"And where's the rest of my pretzel?" said Drake.

"I think I know," said Ursula. "Look!"

The other children looked over at the flamingos. A bright orange flamingo and a brown flamingo with white speckles were standing off to the side while the other flamingos laughed and pointed with their beaks.

"That isn't very nice," said Leo. He felt so bad for the flamingos that he wasn't even upset at missing his own snack. He pulled out a piece of notebook paper and a pen and wrote a new sign:

PLEASE DO NOT LAUGH AT THE FLAMINGOS

"Oh, no!" cried Drake. "Mr. Dapple's on his way back. And the inspectors are with him!"

Indeed, they could see Mr. Dapple and the three inspectors with their white coats walking toward them. Mr. Dapple was lugging a huge barrel.

"We can't let them see the flamingos like this," said Ursula. "We have to do something!"

"They need pink food. And fast!" said Kitty.

"I know!" cried Ursula. "Quick, everyone, what's your classroom job?"

"I'm SBH," said Leo.

"Great!" said Ursula. "You're Shrimp Barrel Helper. You go help Mr. Dapple with the barrel. But not too fast. We need more time! Robin, what about you?"

"I'm CIC."

"Cherry Ices Carrier. I noticed we passed a cart near the last detour sign. Hurry!" Robin ran off, her stomach aching for the poor flamingos. But she knew she had a job to do.

"I'm FF," said Kitty.

"Flamingo Feeder. Kitty, do you think you could figure out how to feed cherry ices to a flamingo?"

"I'm pretty sure I can."

"Excellent! Drake, what's your job?"

"I'm FOF," he said. "I think it must mean 'Fearful of Flamingos.' Since I am."

"Fearful of Flamingos is NOT a job," said Ursula. "You are *Friend* of Flamingos. You keep the flamingos company so they don't get scared. It's got to be pretty frightening to be all different colors like that."

"What will you do?" asked Drake.

"I'm Squirrel Crossing Guard today. I don't want any squirrels to get stepped on with all this running around."

Ursula held up her hand and a squirrel stopped midleap. It was a good thing, too, as Robin was already racing across the path toward the ices cart. Those flamingos needed their cherry ices!

Mr. Dapple and Leo were making slow progress with the barrel of shrimp. Fortunately, Robin was much faster with the cherry ices. Kitty had measured the flamingos' beaks and figured out the best and quickest way to feed them the ices, using an empty cheese popcorn bag and a pencil for poking holes. And Drake was doing a good job being a Friend of Flamingos. He still found them scary, but he thought about how scared they must be, and that made him feel more brave.

When Mr. Dapple, Leo, and the inspectors finally arrived, the flamingos had finished their cherry ices and were back to their normal pink color, if a bit cherry scented.

"Here you go," said Mr. Dapple, dumping the shrimp into the flamingo pen. "53½ pounds of shrimp for you!"

Four of the flamingos began gobbling up the shrimp, but the other two walked away, uninterested.

"That's funny," said Mr. Dapple. "They all seemed so hungry before. I wonder what happened."

Inspector #1 interrupted. "Mr. Dapple, as we were saying, we really must meet with Ms. Font as soon as possible. We have 67 questions that can only be answered by the principal. And that's just so far! The Zoo School simply cannot pass its inspection until we meet with Ms. Font."

Mr. Dapple smiled brightly. "If I see her, I'll let her know."

"Thank you," said the inspectors.

In the distance, the school bell rang. Mr. Dapple said to his students, "Before you all go, please copy down the homework." He held up a portable blackboard.

"HOMEWORK!" groaned the children.

"Ms. Font said it's very important homework, so make sure you copy it correctly," said Mr. Dapple.

"Did she tell you that herself?" asked Ursula.

"No. I've never met her."

Ursula wasn't surprised, but it made her wonder, not for the first time: *Why hasn't anyone ever met Ms. Font?*

Ursula copied the assignment down carefully. She was glad to finally have homework, like at a regular school. She copied it without reading it and then stared in disgust:

HOMEWORK
TOMORROW, WEAR BLACK AND
WHITE STRIPES TO SCHOOL.
(NO POLKA DOTS, PLEASE.)

10

Black and White

Even though the homework was ridiculous, Ursula did it anyway. It was easy. She even borrowed her father's striped socks for extra credit. And it did feel a little like wearing a uniform, which reminded her of her old school.

When she pushed open the door to the classroom that morning, she felt dizzy. She blinked, but what she saw didn't change. Before her was a wall of stripes. She reached out to touch it but felt only air. It wasn't a wall of stripes. Everything in the room was striped! As her eyes began to adjust, she was able to see the outlines of the different shapes. For, indeed, it was the same classroom as always, but everything in it was painted with black and white stripes. The desks were striped. The walls were striped. The windows were striped. The job chart was striped. The pencils were striped.

Ms. Hummingfly was striped. The place where Joseph would be if he had been there was striped. Even the Band-Aid on Robin's knee was striped.

Leo had done the homework by accident—his striped shirt just happened to be on top of the pile. It was his first time ever doing homework, and it wasn't so bad. He thought he might try doing it again sometime.

Kitty was petting the wall and making soft cooing noises, but Ursula hardly noticed. Nothing around here surprised her much anymore.

"Class, please take your seats," said Ms. Hummingfly.

"You mean, please FIND your seats," said Drake. What he thought was his chair turned out to be Leo, and Drake had just sat on him!

"What's with all the stripes?" asked Leo, not too happy about being sat on. "Did Ms. Font decide to spiff up the classroom a bit?"

"Why, no," said Ms. Hummingfly. "The zebra's pen had to have some renovations, so we're using the classroom temporarily. We wanted to make her feel comfortable."

Drake looked around, but he didn't see any zebra. *They must not have brought her in yet,* he thought, relieved.

"But zebras live on the plains of Africa," said Ursula. "It's not all striped there." Sometimes it seemed like this crazy Zoo School made things more complicated on purpose.

"That's true," said Ms. Hummingfly, "but do the African plains have desks and chairs and children?"

"No," said Ursula.

"Do the African plains have fluorescent lights and whirring pencil sharpeners?"

"No," said Ursula.

"Exactly. We didn't think we could convince the zebra that this was Africa, so we thought at least we'd make her feel comfortable. Zebras like stripes. They remind them of their mothers. Also, these stripes make it easy for her to camouflage. Usually zebras camouflage against other zebras, but we have only one. This way she can camouflage against the walls and all of you."

Drake looked over at Kitty, who was still petting the wall. Wait! It wasn't the wall at all. It was a zebra!

"Aaaaaaaahhhhhhhh!" Drake dove under his desk. Or what he thought was his desk.

"Sorry, Leo," he said.

Just then, the door opened and the three white-coated inspectors from L.I.O.N.S. walked in.

"Oh, hello," said Ms. Hummingfly. "Ms. Font didn't tell me you'd be visiting today."

"Do you know where she is?" asked Inspector #1 excitedly. "We haven't been able to find her."

"Are you here to re-inspect the classroom?" asked Ms. Hummingfly. "I know there were some problems the other day. But as you can tell—I mean *smell*—we've taken care of them." She chuckled.

"The classroom?" asked Inspector #3. "Oh, we're not here to inspect the classroom today. We're up to questions 347 through 539. They have to do with lessons. What les-

son will you be teaching today? Reading? Writing? Spelling? Handwriting?"

"Actually, zebras," said Ms. Hummingfly.

"Zebras?" asked Inspector #2, thinking he had heard wrong.

"Yes, zeee-bras," said Ms. Hummingfly as clearly as she could.

"Oh, dear, I don't see anything about zebras in my notebook," said Inspector #2.

"Me, neither," said Inspector #3.

"Our instructions are very clear," said Inspector #1. "They are all spelled out in black and white in our notebooks, and they don't mention lessons about zebras."

"If it helps, I could teach something else," said Ms. Hummingfly. "I don't think the zebra would mind."

"Yes, that would help immensely," said Inspector #2. "Perhaps you could teach a handwriting lesson."

"Anything for the Zoo School," said Ms. Hummingfly, smiling sweetly. "Children, today we are going to work on our handwriting."

The inspectors stood happily at the back of the room. Now things were going according to plan. They each turned to the Handwriting page of their notebooks:

Question 512

Are the handwriting work sheets clear and easy to read?

❑ yes ❑ no

Question 513

Are there nicely dotted lines on which students can practice making their letters? ❑ yes ❑ no

Question 514

Do the students use brightly colored pencil grips? ❑ yes ❑ no

Question 515

Do the students hold their pencils properly? ❑ yes ❑ no

Question 516

Are the pencils nicely sharpened? ❑ yes ❑ no

Question 517

Are the erasers pink and fresh? ❑ yes ❑ no

Question 518

Is the floor free of pencil shavings? ❑ yes ❑ no

Question 519

Are the students sitting up straight? ❑ yes ❑ no

Question 520

Does the teacher use a red marker to correct mistakes?
❑ yes ❑ no

But Ms. Hummingfly was a zookeeper, not a teacher. Everything she knew about teaching, she had learned from Ms. Font, and Ms. Font had never said anything about how to teach handwriting.

Ms. Hummingfly tried to think back to how she had learned handwriting as a child. She shuddered. All she could remember was her teacher making red marks through her *s*'s because they weren't flowing enough.

Then Ms. Hummingfly spotted something strange.

"Ursula, what's that on your pencil?" she asked.

Proudly, Ursula held up her pencil. "It's a pencil grip," she explained. "It's a little plastic triangle for holding your pencil. It's supposed to improve your handwriting."

"How?" asked Ms. Hummingfly.

"I don't know," said Ursula. She had never really thought about that before. "But we had them at my old school."

Ms. Hummingfly shook her head. How bizarre! Oh, what would Ms. Font say to do? Ms. Hummingfly knew Ms. Font had lots of ideas about how to teach children. In fact, it was Ms. Font herself who had come up with the school motto, "Let the Animals Be Your Textbooks!" Why, that was it! Ms. Font would say to let the animals teach the children good handwriting. Why hadn't she thought of that before?

"Children, you can just put those pencils away," said Ms. Hummingfly happily. "We're going to work on our handwriting, all right, but not by *writing*. If you spend your time *writing*, how will your writing improve? You will just keep writing more the same way you already do. What would be the point of that?"

The children nodded. That made sense.

"Please get your coats and line up so we can go about

improving your handwriting the right way, which is by observing the animals, of course."

Everyone put their coats on and lined up. They brought their pencils with them, just in case. Ursula brought her pencil grip with her, too.

The inspectors stared hard at their notebooks. They had observed hundreds of handwriting lessons over the years, and this was not how a handwriting lesson was supposed to look. Where were the work sheets? The papers with dotted lines? The plastic pencil grips in a variety of colors?

Finally, they shrugged, closed their notebooks, and followed the children out the door.

11

SSSnakey SSScript

"So many animals to choose from," said Ms. Hummingfly. "The only question is, Which would be the best, the very best for improving your handwriting?"

"How about the seals?" suggested Kitty. "They use their strong stomach muscles and powerful flippers to swim. Gliding through the water might help our handwriting."

Ms. Hummingfly smiled at Kitty. "That's a good idea, Kitty. But the problem is that your writing would end up all wet. You need to learn how to make DRY flowing lines across the page."

"Birds fly in loop de loops," said Leo. "And the air isn't wet, unless it's raining."

"That's true," said Ms. Hummingfly. "But I wouldn't want your letters to fly away."

"How about worms?" suggested Drake. He didn't think worms would help him with his handwriting, but at least he wasn't scared of them. They were small and didn't move very fast. Drake used to be afraid of worms, but he was feeling braver lately, at least about the smaller animals.

"Worms aren't graceful enough," said Ms. Hummingfly. "But you have given me a great idea, Drake!" And she led the class over to the Snake House.

"Not snakes!" cried Drake.

"Just think of them as worms, only bigger," suggested Ursula.

Drake tried and it helped a little, but not much. He covered his eyes with his hands and headed into the Snake House.

"At least it's nice and warm in here," he said, his eyes still covered.

"It has to be," said Kitty. "Snakes are cold-blooded. They can't make themselves warm, the way people can."

Drake peeked through his fingers. There were snakes everywhere! Black snakes, brown snakes, red-bellied snakes, striped snakes, speckled snakes, hooded snakes, hissing snakes, and lots and lots of slithering snakes.

"Quickly, children!" Ms. Hummingfly called from across the Snake House. "The mmmilk snake is in the mmmiddle of mmmaking some mmmarvelous *mmm*'s!"

Indeed it was. In one smmmooth mmmotion, the red, black, and yellow mmmilk snake mmmade mmmountain after mmmountain until there were mmmillions of mmmar-velous *mmm*'s.

The children copied the snake. They mmmoved smm-moothly across the floor, mmmaking mmmany ammmazing *mmm*'s.

"Mmm!" mouthed the children, but Ms. Hummingfly was already on to the next snake.

"Why is it called a milk snake if it's not white?" Leo asked Kitty. The word *milk* made him a little thirsty. He was looking forward to drinking the peanut-butter milk shake he had in his lunch, but he was also just curious where milk snakes got their name.

"It's because people used to think this kind of snake could drink milk right from a cow. It's not true, of course," Kitty explained.

"Hurry!" cried Ms. Hummingfly. "The diamondback rattler jussst ssswooped a sssplendid *s*. Look, she's doing it again. How sssensssational and sssspectacular!"

The children copied the snake, and now they too were ssslipping and ssssliding the mosssst ssslippery *sss*'s. Drake forgot how ssscary sssnakes were, and Ursula put her pencil grip down near the side of one of the snake pens and found she could make the letters just as nicely without it.

After the children had practiced making all 26 letters, they sat down to rest. When done correctly, handwriting was exhausting!

"Okay, class," said Ms. Hummingfly. "Let's head back to

the classroom. Don't forget your pencils." The children picked up their pencils and lined up.

"I can't find my pencil grip," Ursula said.

"You don't really need it anymore, Ursula, do you? Your handwriting is beautiful without it."

Ursula thought about it. "I guess you're right," she said. "You know, I hope Joseph gets here soon. I think he might have a hard time catching up."

As the class headed toward the door of the Snake House, Drake, feeling more brave, took a last look at the snakes.

"I found your pencil grip," he called to Ursula, pointing. Sure enough, the eastern coral snake was wearing it around its neck.

"It must have picked it up from the edge of its pen where I left it," said Ursula. "I hope it works better for you than it did for me," she called to the snake, giggling.

Ms. Hummingfly clucked her tongue. Already she could see that the snake's movements were less fluid. It was just as she suspected—pencil grips didn't help anyone's handwriting.

The children had worked so hard and had so much fun that they had forgotten all about the inspectors. The inspectors, however, had not forgotten about their inspection. They shook their heads and scribbled furiously in their notebooks. It was time to write another letter to Ms. Font.

Dear Ms. Font,

Today we observed a lesson on handwriting,
an extremely important subject. The lesson
was very confusing and possibly even
permanently damaging to your tender young
students.

As an experienced educator, you must know
that handwriting is best learned sitting at
one's desk, copying letters neatly in
workbooks. It is helpful to use a brightly
colored pencil grip as well.

The lesson today was conducted standing
up in the Snake House, and only one child
had a pencil grip, and a snake almost ate
it. Need we say more?

We suggest that you obtain more
appropriate classroom materials—pencil
grips for the whole class (but not for the
snakes) and other useful, brightly colored
educational materials, such as pattern
cubes, counting bears, and sorting monkeys.

Also, please make an appointment with us
as soon as possible. We need to meet with
you to finish the inspection process. We
know you are very busy, but we must insist.

Sincerely,

Inspector #1, Inspector #2, and Inspector #3
L.I.O.N.S.
(Learned Inspectors of New Schools)

12

Or White and Black?

When Mr. Dapple entered the room, Robin (who was CH) was just finishing cleaning up brown-and-white ice cream drips off the black-and-white-striped floor.

Mr. Dapple smiled. "Wonderful!" he cried. "16 helpers with 32 hands and 160 fingers! You can assist me in giving the zebra her 3½-year-old checkup. It's an important one, you know."

"What kind of checkup does a zebra get?" asked Drake. He found the zebra less scary than he thought, since it blended in so well with everything else.

"I know," said Kitty. "We need to check her hooves and her eyes and her ears. And we should measure her, too—her height and weight."

"And count her stripes," said Mr. Dapple.

Kitty had never heard of that part of a zebra checkup before.

"Why would we need to count her stripes?" she asked.

"To see how many she has, of course!"

Leo said, "But Mr. Dapple. How should we count them? Is she white with black stripes or black with white stripes?"

"Oh! I hadn't thought about that," said Mr. Dapple. "What do you think?"

Robin said, "She is definitely white with black stripes. If you were drawing a picture of a zebra, you would start with a white piece of paper. You wouldn't need to draw any white stripes. You would add black stripes. I'm going to count the black stripes."

Ursula smiled. "What if you were counting her stripes at night?" she asked. "At night, her black stripes wouldn't show, just her white ones. I'm going to count her white stripes." *This was not the sort of thing you got to think about when your math problems came from books, Ursula thought. Only when they were standing in front of you, in black and white.*

Drake was counting slowly to ten. He found both the black stripes and the white stripes scary. But counting made him feel better.

Kitty sighed. The zebra felt so warm and good. She was looking at Kitty with deep brown eyes. *What does it feel like to be a zebra?* wondered Kitty. She wasn't sure counting was going to help her learn more about zebras, not the important things, anyway. But she did like to do things thoroughly. "I'll count all of her stripes," she said.

"Me, too," said Leo. His friends were surprised. Leo usually found the easy way to do a problem. Counting both seemed harder.

When everyone had finished counting, they made a circle in front of the zebra to share their answers.

"I counted 86 white stripes." said Robin.

"I counted 87 black stripes," said Ursula. "I used my calculator."

"Well, I counted ALL the stripes," said Kitty. "There are 87 black stripes and 86 white stripes. That's 173 in all. What did you get?" Kitty asked Leo.

"Zero," said Leo.

"Zero? How could you get zero?" asked Kitty. "Everyone can see the zebra has stripes!"

"Well, I thought about what everyone said. If she's white with black stripes, then she has zero white stripes. If she's black with white stripes, then she has zero black stripes. Zero plus zero is zero. I didn't even have to use a calculator!" He smiled proudly. The others nodded. It made sense, in a Zoo School kind of way.

Mr. Dapple looked horrified. 86? 87? 173? 0? They all seemed right! But how could there be more than one right answer? These were numbers, after all. He ran to the board and began frantically doing his own calculations.

The lunch bell rang, but Mr. Dapple didn't even turn around. Quietly the children tiptoed out of the classroom, leaving him alone with his numbers.

13
Not Everything Is Black and White

The five friends took their lunch boxes and headed over to the Rain Forest Room. It was too cold to eat lunch outside, and the Rain Forest Room was the warmest part of the zoo.

"Poor Mr. Dapple," said Robin as they watched the frogs jump, the lizards leap, and the monkeys swing from branch to branch. "He just can't deal with there being more than one right answer." Robin wished she could make him feel better, but she couldn't think of any medicine that would help.

"Maybe not every question has a right answer and a wrong answer," said Kitty. "Maybe things aren't always that simple."

"Like how there's more than one way to think about counting the zebra's stripes?" said Drake.

"Even the Zoo School itself," said Ursula. "When I first got here, I thought the Zoo School was ridiculous. As clear as black and white. But now, well, some days I'm not sure."

The others started thinking of their own not-black-and-white questions.

"Are all animals scary?" said Drake.

"Is it really best to do as little work as possible?" said Leo.

"Can all problems be solved with a Band-Aid or a cough drop?" said Robin.

"Are facts the best way to learn about animals?" said Kitty.

"And what about Ms. Font?" asked Ursula.

"What do you mean?" said Leo.

"I mean, why hasn't anyone ever seen her?"

"Oh! That's different," said Leo. "That IS black and white—totally obvious. It's because Ms. Font is off enjoying herself. She's probably got her feet up on her desk and is sipping a tropical drink out of a straw right now."

"I don't think so," said Robin. "Maybe she doesn't feel well enough to leave her office and has to lie there in a dark room with a humidifier on, blowing her nose."

"No way!" argued Kitty. "Ms. Font isn't goofing around or sick. She's just very busy. It takes a lot of time to run a zoo and a school. I bet right now she's defleaing a monkey or inspecting the ingrown toenail of a lizard."

"Ew!" said the others.

"That's crazy!" said Drake.

"If you're so smart, why do you think we've never met her?"

"Well . . ." Drake was suddenly embarrassed. "Well . . . I think she might, I mean, it's just an idea, but . . . maybe she's afraid of the animals," he said in a tiny mouse of a voice. It made sense to him before but sounded silly now that he said it out loud.

Kitty and Leo fell over, laughing.

"AFRAID OF THE ANIMALS? The principal of the Zoo School? How could she possibly be scared of the animals?" Kitty asked.

"Yeah, no one who was scared of animals would spend all day in a zoo," said Leo. Then he remembered about Drake, who was now bright red and wishing he hadn't said anything.

"Sorry," said Leo.

"No, I'm sure I'm right," said Kitty. "Ms. Font's simply too busy with the animals to meet with anyone. It's the only thing that makes sense."

"No way. She's probably sunning herself on a porch somewhere. That's the problem."

"SCARED!" insisted Drake.

"SICK!" said Robin.

"OVERWORKED!" argued Kitty.

"BE QUIET!!!!!!" shouted Ursula.

They got quiet.

"See, that's my point," said Ursula. "It seemed so obvious to each of you—black and white. If Joseph were here, he'd probably have his own theory, too. But really, it's not that simple. Maybe you're all right. Maybe she is a frightened, sick, overworked zookeeper who lies around doing nothing. Or maybe none of you is right. Or maybe the answer lies somewhere in the middle."

The others nodded.

"In any case," Ursula said, "as Ms. Font always says, 'If you really want to learn about something, you need to see it for yourself.' I say we go see Ms. Font for ourselves."

The children smiled, glad to be agreeing again. They packed up their lunch boxes, waved goodbye to the monkeys, frogs, and lizards in the Rain Forest Room, and headed toward the principal's office.

"I've never been in a principal's office before," said Kitty, looking up at the stone building in awe. Little elephant statuettes sat in niches around the large oak door. Kitty could tell they were African elephants from their large ears (Asian elephants have much smaller ears), but she didn't say anything. It just didn't seem important now.

"Me, neither," said Leo. "At least, not by choice."

They opened the oak door and entered the outer office. It was bright and sunny but empty except for two gray couches and a coffee table with a bowl of peanuts. To the right hung a portrait of a very old lady with a plaque beneath it that said ZOOLINDA GRAY. To the left was a huge door with MS. FONT, PRINCIPAL written on it in gold type.

Ursula thought she heard a sound coming from inside Ms. Font's office—the sound of a door closing.

"Doesn't Ms. Font have a secretary?" asked Leo, eyeing the bowl of peanuts and licking his lips. "Every principal has a secretary. She's the one who doesn't really look at you while you're waiting for the principal, but you know she's thinking, 'Boy, are you in trouble.'" Leo had a lot of experience with principals at his old school.

"I don't think Ms. Font is that kind of principal," said Robin.

"No one knows what kind of principal she is," said Drake.

They all nodded in agreement.

"Well," said Ursula, "we're about to find out." She knocked on the door marked MS. FONT, PRINCIPAL.

Ursula was wrong. They were not about to find out what kind of principal Ms. Font was. There was no answer.

Just then they heard someone come in behind them.

"Hellooooo, Ms. Font, are you there?" It was the three inspectors, with their notebooks, of course.

"Oh, hello, children. We were looking for Ms. Font. Have you seen her? We really must meet with her to finish our inspection."

"I'm sorry, you just missed her," said Ursula. "She said she had an important matter to take care of."

Inspector #1 sighed. "Ms. Font is always so busy. She must be an awfully good principal."

"We'll have to try again later," said Inspector #2.

"Goodbye, children," said Inspector #3.

As the inspectors let themselves out, Kitty, Leo, Robin, and Drake looked at Ursula, surprised that she had lied. Ursula was surprised herself.

Was it okay to lie to the inspectors?

Was it okay to lie to try to save the Zoo School?

Did she even want to save the Zoo School?

Ursula's feelings about the Zoo School and Ms. Font were certainly not black and white.

14

Counting Bears and Sorting Monkeys

The day was not off to a good start. Robin had a terrible case of the hiccups. Leo hadn't eaten breakfast and wasn't sure if he could make it all the way until snack. And the three inspectors were standing at the back of the room with serious expressions on their faces.

But that wasn't the worst of it. Inside each of the children's desks was a rather large and gooey squid.

The one in Leo's desk was so gross that Leo had completely lost his appetite. He didn't even want to think about what he'd brought for lunch (a peanut-butter-and-orange-marmalade sandwich).

Drake's squid had attached itself upside down to the top

of his desk. Drake took nice deep breaths and did what he could not to run screaming from the classroom. He wished it was his turn to be SCG or HG or even LL. Anything to get him out of the classroom!

Robin's squid was so disgusting that looking at it scared the hiccups right out of her. But she would have traded it for the hiccups anytime.

The other children weren't too excited about looking down at the slimy squids, either. Ursula's had somehow oozed down one of the legs of her desk. Gross!

Only Kitty found the squid fascinating, with its toothed tongue (which she knew was called a radula) and finned tail. She looked over at Joseph's desk. The chair, of course, was empty, but the desk itself contained a particularly large squid. *Poor Joseph,* she thought. *He's missing all the fun!*

The door flew open and in came Ms. Hummingfly, pushing a large cart that held two humongous boxes. Mr. Dapple helped her unload them. The boxes stood at the front of the room like giant birthday presents.

"What's in the boxes?" asked Drake. He was so excited, he forgot all about the squid inside his desk.

"I don't know," said Ms. Hummingfly, "but Ms. Font asked that I bring them over right away." She waved goodbye and left.

Mr. Dapple adjusted his glasses and read the tiny words on the sides of the boxes. "This one says COUNTING BEARS, and that one says SORTING MONKEYS."

The inspectors beamed with pleasure. Finally! Some real

learning would take place. They had already marked *yes* next to question 642. *Do the students use a variety of appropriate objects for counting and sorting?*

"Oh, I know what those are," said Ursula. "We had them in my old school. They're for math. Counting bears are little plastic bears that come in all different colors. You can play counting games with them and do problems, like, *If there are 7 yellow bears and 12 blue bears, how many are there in all?*"

"I remember those bears," said Kitty. "They're boring. They're not even anatomically correct. They don't have thick fur or loose skin like real bears. They don't have five toes on each foot, and they have no claws at all. They're not like any kind of real bears in the whole world!" Kitty looked down at her squid. She found it much more interesting than pretend bears.

"Yes, but at least they're part of *regular* school," said Ursula "And look! The box is so big, there must be thousands in there! We can spend all day counting them." As Ursula said it, her stomach dropped—and not because of the squids. She should be excited about counting thousands of the plastic bears they have at regular school, but she found herself wishing she could walk around the zoo and see real bears instead. Maybe Zoo School wasn't all that bad.

They looked at the other box.

"What are sorting monkeys?" asked Leo. He might have had them in his old school, but he'd never paid much attention.

"I get to hand them out," said Ursula. "I'm Monkey Monitor (MM) today."

"I know what sorting monkeys are," said Drake. "They come in different colors, too, and even different sizes, and they're not scary at all. You can sort out all the green ones. Or all the orange ones. Or all the big ones. Or all the—"

Just then, the box burst open.

"—alive ones!" cried Drake. Suddenly the room was filled with monkeys of all different colors and sizes—big brown monkeys with red rumps, furry white-and-black monkeys with long tails, tiny yellowish monkeys, and more!

The inspectors just stared with their mouths hanging open, but the children got right to work. Ursula didn't have to help pass them out after all.

"Does anyone have any monkeys with blue cheeks?" yelled Leo, holding one he had caught.

"I've got one like that!" shouted Robin above the commotion. The blue-cheeked monkey was kindly scratching her shoulder, which was rather itchy.

"Those are mandrills," called Kitty. "They're among the largest monkeys, weighing up to 90 poun— Oh, heck! They're beautiful, aren't they?" She stroked the nearest mandrill and picked a flea out of its soft fur.

"I'm going to count the monkeys I'm not scared of," said Drake. "One . . . two . . . three . . . four . . ." He was pleased that there were so many.

Surprisingly, Ursula wasn't disappointed that the monkeys were real instead of plastic. After all, real monkeys were much more fun to count. For instance, she had just spotted three monkeys grabbing the inspectors' notebooks with their tails.

"That's a spider monkey, a woolly monkey, and a howler," said Mr. Dapple over the sounds of the monkeys' screeching. "They are all New World monkeys. The Old World Monkeys, such as baboons, langurs, and macaques, can't use their tails to grasp objects like that."

Everyone was so busy sorting monkeys that no one thought to count the inspectors. All three of them had left hurriedly without their notebooks. They didn't need them. They knew just what their letter to Ms. Font would say.

Dear Ms. Font,

After watching today's lesson (in which real monkeys took the place of perfectly good plastic ones), we have no choice but to CLOSE THE ZOO SCHOOL IMMEDIATELY. As of tomorrow, all students must attend other schools.

Please expect us in your office at 9:00 a.m. sharp tomorrow morning so that you can sign the appropriate papers. At that time we will also do our final inspection to make sure that the school has been properly closed down.

Sincerely,

Inspector #1, Inspector #2, and Inspector #3
L.I.O.N.S.
(Learned Inspectors of New Schools)

15

The New Student

I should be happy about this, thought Ursula as she walked toward her old school the next morning. She imagined the day in front of her, filled with looking things up in her dictionary and counting plastic animals. It was what she used to want. But somehow, her feet seemed to move more slowly with each step.

Robin's stomach hurt, but she didn't think the nurse at her old school would be able to help. She recognized this stomachache. It was the same kind she had the time those poor flamingos turned the wrong colors.

Leo walked toward his old school, but all he could think about was his classroom job at the Zoo School. *I'm Snack Helper today. If I'm not there, who will feed the animals?*

Kitty was thinking about the animals, too. Not how many spots they had or how much they weighed. No, Kitty was thinking about how good it felt just to see them every morning. Giving the zebra a good-morning hug or patting the hippo hello. The school she was going to had lots of books about animals. But it wasn't the same. After all, you couldn't pet a book.

Drake was feeling a bit scared. Scared of what a day would be like with no animals. But he had to be brave.

Or did he?

An hour later, Ursula, Kitty, Robin, Leo, and Drake were standing in front of the main gate to the zoo, staring at a big sign:

ZOO SCHOOL CLOSED
BY ORDER OF L.I.O.N.S.

The five students knew what they had to do. They slipped under the sign and through the gate and headed directly for their classroom.

Was it okay not to go to their old schools, where they were expected?

Was it okay to sneak back into the Zoo School?

Yes.

The animals had to be cared for!

It was as clear as black and white.

They pushed open the door to the classroom and stared sadly at what they saw—and what they didn't see. All the bears had been counted and taken to their dens. All the monkeys had been sorted and moved to the Monkey House. The desks were empty as well. The room was very, very boring. At least the job chart was still there. The children checked their jobs. They wanted to be ready to help the animals.

The clock struck 9:00, but no bell rang. The children began to get ready for their day anyway. There were squirrels to see safely across the paths, hungry animals to feed, lonely animals to greet.

At 9:01, the door burst open. Breathless, Ms. Hummingfly ran in.

The children were shocked. They hadn't expected any teachers today.

"I was hoping you'd come," Ms. Hummingfly cried. "We need your help! The inspectors are waiting in Ms. Font's office. They are insisting on meeting with Ms. Font today, but she is nowhere to be found. All the zookeepers are needed to look for her. It's our only chance. If she would just meet with them and they could see how wonderful she is, maybe they'll reopen the school. And meanwhile, Joseph has just arrived, and there's no one to greet him or to tell him the sad news."

"I'll go," said Ursula. "I'm NSG, New Student Greeter."

"I'll go, too!" said Leo. "I'm Snack Helper. I bet Joseph is hungry after his long trip."

"I'm Paper Passer. I can help Joseph carry his notebooks," said Kitty.

"I'm Squirrel Crossing Guard," said Robin. "I better go along. Just in case."

"I'll go, too," said Drake.

"What's your job?" asked Robin.

"MM."

"What does Monkey Monitor have to do with welcoming a new student?" asked Kitty.

"Probably nothing, but I know how scary it is to be in a new place. I want to help."

Ms. Hummingfly smiled at her students. "Thank you! You should be able to find Joseph by the main gate. I haven't seen him yet, but I think that's where he was dropped off. I hear he's having a tough time."

"Don't worry! We'll take care of him," the five students cried, running out of the classroom.

Poor Joseph, thought Ursula as she led the way. She remembered how much she used to miss her old school. She wondered if that was how Joseph was feeling now.

Poor Joseph, thought Leo. He was probably hungry and tired after his long trip. Leo knew all about being hungry and tired.

Poor Joseph, thought Drake. He hoped Joseph wasn't afraid of animals. But if he was, Drake would help him. Drake was an expert at getting over fears.

Poor Joseph, thought Kitty. Perhaps a nice bear hug would make him feel more comfortable at his new school.

Poor squirrels! thought Robin. The children were in such a rush that it was quite dangerous for the squirrels. She held up her hand in the stop position a moment too late, and someone stepped on the very end of a small gray squirrel's tail. Robin put a Band-Aid on it. Then she ran after her friends.

When they reached the main gate, there was a lot of commotion. A big truck was there, and the driver was having trouble with a large box.

"I'm supposed to deliver this," the truck driver told the children. "I've been waiting here more than an hour, but no one's come for it yet."

"The zookeepers are very busy today," explained Drake. "We don't know anything about a delivery. We're just here to meet Joseph."

"Joseph? Oh, you must mean Joey. He's in here," said the truck driver, pointing to the label on the box. Indeed, it said JOEY.

The children looked at each other with surprise. New students usually arrived on school buses, not in boxes. But then again, Ms. Hummingfly had said he was coming from very far away.

"Sign here," said the truck driver. Ursula wrote her name on the form. After Ms. Hummingfly's wonderful snake lesson, Ursula now had extremely nice handwriting.

The truck driver plunked down the box labeled JOEY, jumped back in his truck, yelled, "Good luck!" and drove away quickly.

"I wonder why we would need luck?" said Drake.

"Let's not just stand here," said Ursula. "We need to get Joseph out of that box!"

"Maybe we should call him Joey. That must be his nickname," said Robin, pointing at the label on the box.

"Don't worry, Joey, we'll have you out in a minute," Leo shouted into an air hole.

Just then, the box jumped.

"Whirling wallabies!" cried Kitty. "Joey is strong."

"Now, Joey," said Ursula. "Hold still so we can get this box opened." She bent down and peeked into the air hole. "Hopping hyenas! Joey is furry!"

The other children bent down to get a peek, too, but the box had started hopping again.

"Do you think it's filled with monkeys again?" asked Drake bravely. "I am Monkey Monitor today."

"I think Joey is in there. I'm just not sure WHAT Joey is," said Leo.

The box was hopping away at a terrific pace. The chase was on!

The children followed the box around the Seal Pool (three times), the Snake House (five times), and Flamingo Lake (twice). By the time they had circled the Zoo School classroom (thankfully, just once), they were exhausted.

"We'll never catch him," said Ursula.

"Yes, we will!" said Leo, speeding up. As swiftly as a hawk soaring after a mouse, Leo leaped through the air and landed on the box, tackling it right in front of the Elephant Yard.

"Hooray!" cried the others as they dragged their tired bodies over to where Leo and the box lay in a heap.

Very carefully, Leo climbed off the box. It was a bit smushed.

"I hope I didn't hurt him," said Leo. "I'm too scared to look."

"I'll look!" said Drake. He knew that sometimes you have to do things even if you're scared.

The others gathered around as Drake slowly opened the box.

There was no new student in the box. Instead, at the bottom, blinking in the bright sunlight, was a tiny furry animal, shaking with fear.

16
classroom Renovations

"It's a joey!" cried Kitty.

"Yes, we know that's his name," said Leo. "But what is he?"

"Joey isn't just his name. It's what he IS. A joey is a baby kangaroo."

"He's so cute!" said Drake, lifting him out gently. "How could I ever have been afraid of animals?" He held the fuzzy joey against his chest.

"Poor little thing," said Kitty. "Kangaroos are marsupials, so they stay in their mother's pouches a long time after they're born. This one is about a year old, I'd say—old enough to be out of his mother's pouch, but he must miss his mother very much."

"Where's he from?" asked Robin.

"He's an eastern gray kangaroo," said Kitty. "They live in

the woodlands of Australia. They stay in the shade of the woods all day and in the evening come out to eat grass."

Leo, Drake, Robin, and Kitty were all busy petting the scared little kangaroo, but Ursula had a funny feeling in her stomach—not exactly stomach butterflies, but maybe distant cousins of stomach butterflies. It was the feeling you get when you're being watched. Carefully she looked around.

She saw the old elephant out in its yard. It was chewing on some hay and looking over at them with huge, thoughtful eyes. High above the elephant, Ursula could see a window. That must be the window in Ms. Font's office, she realized. She squinted and could just make out three pairs of eyes peering at the children. Perched above the eyes were familiar hats. The inspectors! For a moment, Ursula's distant cousins of stomach butterflies got worse. She wondered whether Ms. Font had been found and whether she had convinced L.I.O.N.S. to reopen the Zoo School. She wondered if she and her friends would get in trouble for being at the Zoo School today instead of at their old schools. But then she looked back at her friends caring for the poor little kangaroo, and her other thoughts vanished. Joey needed *all* of their help!

Leo's stomach growled. "I think it's lunchtime," he said.

"Leo," scolded Robin, "can't you think of anyone besides yourself?"

"I didn't mean for *me*," said Leo. "I meant, maybe the kangaroo is hungry. Maybe eating something would make him feel better."

"Sorry, Leo. That's good thinking," said Robin. "What do baby kangaroos eat?"

"Not shrimp," said Drake. "We don't want him to turn pink!"

Kitty shook her head. "Kangaroos eat grass and small plants."

The others smiled. That was easy enough. There was grass all over the zoo!

Carefully, Leo placed the joey in a nearby patch of grass.

He began to graze right away. A few minutes later he looked much happier.

"But he'll need a place to stay for the night," said Ursula. "And the zoo doesn't have any other kangaroos."

"I guess he could stay in the Small Mammals House," said Kitty, "with the possums and yellow-footed marsupial mice. They're all marsupials from Australia."

"I wish there was a way to give him more special attention, though," said Ursula. "After all, the Zoo School is a strange new place for a joey."

"I know!" said Drake. "He can stay in our classroom. It's not like we've never had any animals in there before. And Joey is the 'new student,' after all."

"Drake," said Kitty. "I don't think MM stands for Monkey Monitor today. I think your job is Marsupial Monitor." Drake smiled.

The other children began gathering up more grass and some sticks and moss. They wanted to make the classroom as comfortable as possible for a kangaroo. By now Joey was feeling better and hopped along beside them.

Ursula took one more look back toward Ms. Font's office. The elephant was still in the yard, looking sleepy but happy. The window above was empty now. Ursula shrugged. She couldn't worry about L.I.O.N.S. or the school or even herself. She had a joey to care for!

Back at the classroom, the students worked together to make a good environment for Joey. Kitty told them everything she knew about the animals of the Australian woodlands. Many of them were marsupials, like Joey, and some of them lived right here at the zoo. Ursula looked up *Australia* in her encyclopedia and made lists of Australian plants that she had seen around the zoo.

Leo filled the classroom with baby eucalyptus trees. Robin replaced all the chairs with strong acacia bushes. She didn't want Joey falling off any chairs and getting hurt.

Ursula pulled down the big map above the blackboard. She found Australia and put a gold star on it.

Kitty carried in some possums and yellow-footed marsupial mice from the Small Mammals House and made them comfortable in the desks and on the floor.

Drake went to the Bear Den and brought back some koala bears. According to Kitty, koalas were marsupials from Australia and, despite their name, were not really bears at all!

When they were done, they looked around proudly. Ursula said, "As Ms. Font always says, 'If a little of a good thing is good, then a lot of a good thing is even better.'" It was certainly true. Koala bears clung to the trunks of the baby eucalyptus trees. Possums crept over the branches, tiny babies clinging to their backs. Golden acacia blossoms bloomed. High above, kookaburras flew merrily, singing their names.

And down on the woodland-classroom floor, Joey hopped contentedly around the room, looking very much at home.

All the children much preferred sharing their classroom with Joey to having squids or bats or even fish in their desks. Ursula thought he was even better than the class guinea pig they had at her old school. He was much cuter and more exciting, the way he hopped all over.

At 1:00, the children ate their lunch. They sat on acacia bushes, under eucalyptus trees. Leo gave Joey the lettuce off his turkey-lettuce-and-peanut-butter sandwich. Kitty wiped the lettuce bits off Joey's chin.

At 2:00, the children decided to do some schoolwork. After all, they didn't want to get behind. They counted how many hops it took Joey to get across the room (3). They measured Joey's height (22 inches), counted his toes (5 on each front foot, 4 on each hind foot), and learned to spell *kangaroo* backward (*ooragnak*). And they worked on the job chart. They changed the hook label from Joseph to Joey (Joey looked much more like a Joey than a Joseph!), and they made a job to hang on his hook. It said CK (Class Kangaroo). They weren't sure exactly what the job would require, but they knew Joey would be perfect for it.

At 3:00, they dismissed themselves. They kissed Joey good night on his furry little head, waved goodbye to the possums, yellow-footed marsupial mice, and koala bears, made their way through the eucalyptus trees, and closed the door.

Had Ms. Font met with the inspectors from L.I.O.N.S.? Would there ever again be a Zoo School? The children had been so busy caring for Joey that they forgot to even think about these questions. Their classroom was so full of kangaroo that there was no room for worries or the distant cousins of stomach butterflies.

17

Itty-Bitty-Cutesy-Wootsy-Oogy-Woogy

Joey had a wonderful night in his new home, but in the morning, he was happy to see the children and bounded (in only 2 hops) right over to them. At 9:00 the bell didn't ring, but the door opened, and Ms. Hummingfly walked in, looking very sad. She sat down sadly on an acacia bush and sighed very sadly. Sadly, she looked over at Joey and said sadly, "Oh, hello. You must be the new student. Welcome to the Sad—I mean, Zoo—School. Sorry you won't get to stay." She sighed again, with great sadness.

"Oh, no!" said Ursula. The news was clearly not good. Ms. Hummingfly was so sad that she hadn't even noticed that Joey was a joey and not a child. Or that the classroom looked like the Australian woodland. A kookaburra landed on Ms. Hummingfly's head, and she brushed it off as if it were a fly.

"She didn't show up," Ms. Hummingfly said. "Ms. Font always says, 'Never put things off until tomorrow,' but it IS tomorrow and Ms. Font didn't show up. Mr. Dapple and I looked all night. We looked in the Monkey House and in the Zebra Pen. We looked in the Small Mammals House and near the Seal Pool. But it's hard to find someone you've never met. We called, 'Ms. Font! Ms. Font!' but she didn't answer.

"Mr. Dapple thinks that something awful must have happened to her. I am holding on to hope that something awful did NOT happen to her. But in any case, we both agree that something awful has happened to the Zoo School. It is closed forever. Oh, poor Joseph! How will he ever learn about animals?" Ms. Hummingfly gestured toward Joey without looking at him.

"But Joey IS an animal," said Leo.

"Leo, don't call people names, especially at a time like this," Ms. Hummingfly scolded. Then she exclaimed, "Oh, my goodness, I almost forgot why I came! You all need to leave the Zoo School right away, before the inspectors come back. We expect them any minute for their final inspection to make sure we closed down everything properly. You and I and Ms. Font would all get in a lot of trouble if they found you here. You're not supposed to be at a school that L.I.O.N.S. has ordered closed. Oh, if only Ms. Font was here to help!"

115

Just then, the door opened.

It wasn't Ms. Font.

It was the three inspectors.

"Uh, I wish I could stay," cried Ms. Hummingfly, "but I need to feed Ms. Font to the fish and try to find the seals. Wait, no! I mean, I need to feed the seals to Ms. Font and try to find the fish. No! Oh, you know what I mean!" She ran out the door in a fluster.

"What in the world is going on in here?" cried Inspector #1, looking around.

"We can explain——" said Ursula.

"This school was supposed to be closed! This classroom should be empty. Instead, it is filled with children and—ugh!—rodents!"

"Actually, they're not rodents," explained Leo. "They're marsupials. Those big ones are possums, and the little ones are yellow-footed marsupial mice."

"And how on earth did these pigeons get in here?" cried Inspector #2, wiping his hair.

"You mean the kookaburras?" asked Robin. "We brought them, to keep the kangaroo company."

"I thought I smelled something funny," said Inspector #3.

"You children brought these animals in here?" exclaimed Inspector #1. "Not only is this school closed forever, but you children are in very, very, very, VERY big trou— Oh, my!"

Inspector #1 never finished her sentence, because just then she spotted Joey. Kitty was holding him and nuzzling the top of his head with her chin.

"Oh, my, is that the kangaroo?" asked Inspector #1. "I've never seen one up close before."

"He's a joey. That's what you call a baby kangaroo," said Kitty. "Do you want to hold him?"

"Well, I don't know," said Inspector #1.

"Don't be scared," said Drake. "He's very friendly." Inspector #1 put her notebook down, and Kitty put the joey into her arms.

"Isn't he sweet?" said Inspector #1.

"What an itty-bitty-cutesy-wootsy-oogy-woogy little kangaroo!" crooned Inspector #2, reaching out to touch Joey's velvety nose. "Ouch! He bit my finger!"

Robin examined the inspector's finger. "Don't worry. That was just a nibble," she said. "You don't need a Band-Aid."

"Joey doesn't usually bite people," explained Leo. "He must be hungry."

"What does he eat?"

"Mostly grass and other plants," said Leo, passing a few blades of grass to the inspector.

"Where did you learn so much about kangaroos?" asked Inspector #1.

Ursula pointed at the banner. "As Ms. Font always says, 'Let the animals be your textbooks.'"

"Have you actually met Ms. Font?" asked Inspector #3. "We still have so many questions to answer about the principal." She held up a page of her inspector notebook. The children gathered around to look.

Question 18

Is the principal neatly dressed? ❏ yes ❏ no

Question 19

Does the principal care about the school? ❏ yes ❏ no

Question 20

Is the principal well organized? ❏ yes ❏ no

Question 21

Is the principal intelligent and well educated? ❏ yes ❏ no

Question 22

Does the principal encourage students to take good care of their textbooks and other materials? ❏ yes ❏ no

Question 23

Describe your overall impression of the principal upon completion of the in-person interview.

"We've never met Ms. Font, either," said Ursula. "But I bet she would be happy to know we're taking such good care of our textbooks." She smiled, pointing at Joey.

"I bet she would," said Inspector #2, smiling back. The inspectors checked off *yes* next to question 22.

"Well, I bet Ms. Font is NOT happy that the Zoo School is closed," said Leo.

"No," agreed Inspector #3. "I expect she is not."

Suddenly, Ursula had an idea.

"How can you be so sure?" Ursula said. "I mean, Ms. Font never even bothered to meet with L.I.O.N.S. Maybe she's lazy.

Maybe she doesn't like animals. Maybe she doesn't like children. Maybe she doesn't even care about the Zoo School!"

"Ursula!" cried Robin. "How can you say such things?" The children all stared at Ursula with shocked expressions. They loved the Zoo School! Didn't Ursula love it, too?

"I must disagree with the young lady," Inspector #1 said, pointing at Ursula. "Ms. Font could not have created a school that would foster such kind and caring students unless she herself cared a great deal about it." The inspectors checked off *yes* next to question 19 in their notebooks.

"Well, maybe she cares about the school," said Ursula, "but she must not be a very good principal. Don't you think a good, well-organized principal would have met with the inspectors?"

"On the contrary," said Inspector #3. "I think Ms. Font must be a wonderful principal! She must be very well organized to be able to run this school so well without anyone ever meeting her face-to-face." The inspectors checked off *yes* next to question 20.

"And she must be very smart, too," said Inspector #2, reading question 21, "because of all the brilliant things people say that she always says."

Ursula smiled. "I guess you're right," she said.

There followed a very nice moment. In this nice moment, the children looked around. The inspectors looked around. Even the joey looked around. And all of them appreciated how very fine the Zoo School and its principal were.

It was too bad the nice moment was about to end.

18

A Big Gray Area

Inspector #1 sighed. "What a shame that such a fine school has to close," she said, "but that's the way it is." She took something out of the back of her notebook and began to unfold it. It was a huge sign that said CLOSED.

Drake mustered all his courage. "But now that you see how great the Zoo School *and* Ms. Font are," he said, "isn't there some way you could reopen the school?"

The inspectors sighed.

"I wish we could," said Inspector #2. "But there's a problem. Clearly, Ms. Font and the Zoo School have done a marvelous job of educating their students. You know so many facts about animals, and you have shown yourselves to be very smart, responsible, caring students."

"But then what's the problem?"

"The problem is that we have rules and procedures to follow when we inspect schools. And it is standard procedure for us to meet with the principal." She held up her notebook. "See, it's all spelled out right here in black and white."

Ursula smiled. "You know," she said. "Not everything is black and white."

"It's not?" asked the inspectors.

Everyone started talking at once.

"Oh, no!" said Leo. "Take a zebra, for instance. Is it white with black stripes or black with white stripes? You could say it doesn't have any stripes at all!"

"No stripes?" asked Inspector #1.

"And what about an invisible lion?" Kitty was saying. "Just because it's invisible doesn't mean you can't draw a picture of it. You just have to work a little harder."

"Did you say *invisible* lion?" asked Inspector #2.

"Or snakes," said Robin. "So what if they don't have hands? They can still have lovely handwriting!"

"I guess I see what you mean, sort of," said Inspector #3, scratching her head.

"Or take that elephant, even," said Ursula, pointing out the window. "What do you think we could learn from that elephant?"

Everyone looked out the window at the old elephant moving slowly around in her yard.

Inspector #1 shook her head. "Elephants. What an easy

life!" she said. "Just standing around all day, chewing hay and turning around when someone tries to take their picture."

"Oh! That's not what I see at all," said Inspector #2, squinting. "I see a poor old elephant, so bored at being penned up like that. I feel terrible for her."

"Really?" said Inspector #3. "To me, that elephant seems deep in thought. I wonder if she has some instinctive understanding of what a predicament the Zoo School is in right now."

"As I was saying," said Ursula. "Not everything is black and white. Sometimes there's a big gray area!" She pointed at the elephant and giggled.

"Maybe you don't really need to meet with Ms. Font after all," said Kitty.

"Or answer questions in notebooks," said Robin.

"Or count how many plastic bears or pencil grips we have," added Leo.

"Real bears *are* more interesting," agreed Inspector #1, cuddling with a koala. Kitty could have told her that the koala is not actually related to bears despite its name. But she was too worried about the Zoo School to think of it.

"Maybe you can look around the Zoo School and *just know* that it's a good school," said Ursula. "Maybe you can *just know* that Ms. Font is an excellent principal."

"We do feel as if we already know her," said Inspector #2.

"Maybe sorting real monkeys isn't the worst idea," said Inspector #3 as she counted Joey's 18 adorable toes.

"And perhaps snakes are a good subject for a handwriting lesson," said Inspector #1, admiring the paws of the sweetest little yellow-footed marsupial mouse.

"I must say I loved those dark walnut desks that you used to have in here," said Inspector #2, relaxing on an acacia bush.

"I hereby call an emergency meeting of the L.I.O.N.S. at the ice cream cart in five minutes," announced Inspector #3.

By the time the students had finished eating their own snack (salted popcorn and peanuts for the children, salted dandelion heads for Joey), a final letter—a happy letter—was posted on Ms. Font's office door:

Dear Ms. Font,

Today we had the pleasure of watching your
students demonstrate extraordinary knowledge
and care learned at the Zoo School. And
they saved an itty-bitty-cutesy-wootsy-
oogy-woogy baby kangaroo!

While it is highly out of the ordinary
for us to bend the rules, we have no choice
but to overlook the fact that we have never
met you. Now that we know where—and how—to
look, we see that your wonderful ideas are
all over the Zoo School—in the banners on
the classroom walls, in the voices of the
students, and in the wonderful care they
took of the itty-bitty-cutesy-wootsy-oogy-
woogy baby kanga—. Yes, well, as we were
saying . . . We have also chosen to
disregard the fact that the tests were so
. . . blank. While none of the questions
were answered correctly, at least none of
them were answered incorrectly. As you
probably like to say, "It all depends on
how you look at it!"

Therefore, we are pleased to announce that
L.I.O.N.S. grants the Zoo School its Super-
Duper Top-Rated Gold Seal of Approval!

Sincerely,

Inspector #1, Inspector #2, and Inspector #3
L.I.O.N.S.
(Learned Inspectors of New Schools)

19
An Elephant Never Forgets

The next morning, the Zoo School was officially reopened and the whole class was back. Everyone was so excited that Joey wasn't the only one hopping around the classroom. Leo hopped (14 times) across the room. And Drake hopped higher than a baby eucalyptus tree. "Hop hop hooray!" they cried.

When they were done celebrating, Ms. Hummingfly said, "Let's get to work. After all, as Ms. Font always says, 'Never put off learning something new.'" Everyone nodded.

"Let me just put away this map of Australia so I can write the assignment on the blackboard." She pulled a string, and the map sprang back on its roll. Everyone stared in amazement because behind the map, a message was written in uneven handwriting on the blackboard:

WOULD URSULA, LEO, KITTY,
ROBIN, AND DRAKE PLEASE
COME TO MY OFFICE DIRECTLY?
THANK YOU,
Ms. FONT

No one said a word as the five students pushed back their acacia bushes, squeezed in between the eucalyptus trees—careful not to step on any yellow-footed marsupial mice—and made their way out of the classroom.

The children had been to Ms. Font's office before, of course, but this time was different. They were so nervous, they hardly noticed the two large gray couches or the portrait of Zoolinda Gray. They went straight to the door with the little gold plaque that said MS. FONT, PRINCIPAL. Bravely, Drake knocked on the door.

A booming voice called, "Come in."

Together they pushed open the huge door and walked inside.

There was no sign of Ms. Font. Curiously, the children examined the gigantic things in this gigantic room.

The walls were covered floor to ceiling with books and magazines. There were books about animals and books about schools, and there were hundreds of copies of *Zooey!* magazine.

In the middle of the room stood an enormous oak desk.

A gigantic telephone sat on one side of it, and pencils the size of baseball bats stood in a barrel next to the desk. Behind the desk was a humongous leather chair with its back turned toward them.

"Hello, children," came a large voice from the large shadow on the large chair. She sounded so kind and gentle! The children couldn't believe they had been worried about meeting her. They felt as if they'd known her a long time already.

"Hello, Ms. Font," the children said to the back of the chair.

"You must call me Ella," she said. "Please excuse me for not turning around. I'm quite private, you know."

They knew.

"I wanted to thank you for saving the Zoo School."

The children smiled proudly.

"And I feel that I owe you some sort of explanation. I know it may seem that it would have been easier if I had simply met with the inspectors. It may have seemed that I was being selfish. But when you hear my story, you will see that is not the case, and that, as you know, not everything is black and white.

"You see, for many, many years this zoo was run by a zookeeper named Zoolinda Gray. Her picture is hanging in the outer office. Maybe you saw it on your way in? Zoolinda was a superb zookeeper. She knew so much about animals. She even founded the magazine *Zooey!* (short for Zoolinda, of course).

"But more importantly, Zoolinda loved animals, and her favorite was the elephant. That's why her office was attached to the back of the Elephant Yard, as mine is. How Zoolinda loved that elephant! She grew her own extra-nutritious peanuts for the elephant to eat. She created a recipe for a mud bath that went on extra muddy but washed off easily.

"Just as Zoolinda loved animals, she also loved children. It was her idea that children and animals have a lot in common and that learning about animals would make children nicer and smarter and, eventually, better grownups. Her great dream was to start the Zoo School, in which the students would learn about animals and about themselves, not just from reading books but from the actual animals.

"But alas, Zoolinda was too old to realize her dream of creating the Zoo School. She knew she had to find someone to carry out her dream, someone who would care about it as much as she did.

"Every day she worried about who she could ask. She would sit in the Elephant Yard next to her favorite elephant and talk and talk and talk. The elephant never said a word, of course, but she listened. *This* zookeeper was more interested in numbers than in animals or children. *That* zookeeper was too silly, and so on. Who would be able to understand the needs of animals and children well enough? To care enough? Zoolinda would sigh and say she had to make the decision soon. After all, as Zoolinda always said, 'Never put things off until tomorrow.'

"One day, Zoolinda turned right to me—er—the elephant and said, 'You know, I wish *you* could take over the creation of the Zoo School. For years I have been sharing all my ideas about children and schools and animals with you. I can see in your eyes you've been listening. And as the saying goes, "An elephant never forgets." Elephant, will you help me?'

"And at that moment a remarkable thing happened. The elephant realized that it was true. She remembered every word Zoolinda had ever said to her about schools and children and zoos. And she knew English perfectly, too, from listening to Zoolinda all those years.

"The elephant didn't hesitate. She cleared her humongous throat and in perfect English said, 'Zoolinda, you have been a true friend and keeper to me, and I would be happy to take over the Zoo School for you. I have been listening to your wonderful ideas for years now, and I feel that I know all I need to about zoos, schools, children—and, of course, elephants. I even have a motto for the Zoo School: Let the Animals Be Your Textbooks!'"

Ms. Font turned around now, unsure what the children's reaction would be. She saw their wide smiles. Through her long tusks, Ms. Font smiled back.

20
A New Job Chart

Facing the children now, Ms. Font went on with her story. "Just one year later, the Zoo School opened. Zoolinda never got to see it, but I know she would have loved it." Ms. Font wiped a humongous tear from her gigantic eye.

"When I first started planning the Zoo School, I tried to hire people to help me—an assistant principal, a secretary, some regular teachers. But the interviews didn't go very well. Instead of sitting down and talking to me about the job, each person ran away yelling, 'Help! Help! The elephant has escaped!'

"Next, I tried to get the animals to help me, but that didn't work out, either. The monkeys were too skittish, and I was constantly tripping on their banana peels. The seals got everything all wet. And the tigers! Let's just say they weren't team players. That's when I realized I'd have to run it all myself—the zoo and the school—but from behind the scenes.

"The zookeepers have been just wonderful, of course. They already knew how to take care of the animals, and I figured it's not that different caring for children, so I made them the teachers as well. They don't seem to mind never meeting with me face-to-face. I just leave them notes telling them what to do. Running the school hasn't been easy, but I've managed pretty well—except for this L.I.O.N.S. inspection, that is. It was just too much for me, with its constant demands that I meet with those people in *person*. As if I could meet with anyone in *person!*

"And I am embarrassed to say that for the first time, I even mixed up the *zoo* and the *Zoo School*—thinking all year that Joseph was a new student instead of a new animal. I want to thank the five of you—for saving Joey *and* for saving the Zoo School!

"And I also want to thank you for reminding me of Zoolinda, each in your own way. Drake, for your bravery and sensitivity to others. Leo, for your incredible appetite—for food (Zoolinda could eat more peanut butter than a herd of elephants!)—but also for life. Kitty, for your incredible knowledge about animals. Robin, for taking care of others— children and animals. And Ursula, for your ability to get things done and to know what needs to get done.

"Thank you all for helping me. And just as Zoolinda said

to me, 'Will you help me?' so I say to you today, 'Will you help me more?' Because I do need your help."

There is a new job chart hanging at the Zoo School. It's not in the classroom. It's in Ms. Font's office. And it's a different kind of job chart. There are only six jobs, and they don't switch every day:

ZOO SCHOOL OFFICE JOB CHART
MS. FONT—P
KITTY—AP
LEO—CC
DRAKE—GC
ROBIN—SN
URSULA—AD

Ms. Font is still the principal, of course, but with so many wonderful helpers, she is able to spend some time "just standing around being an elephant" as well. The work isn't challenging, but she enjoys it.

As Assistant Principal, Kitty is in charge of what the students study. She makes sure everyone learns lots of facts about the animals as well as how to be a good friend. She also contributes occasional articles to the fine magazine *Zooey!* She has one coming up soon on the effects of sugar on flamingos.

As Chief Cook, Leo orders lunch and snack for the students as well as the animals. He always makes sure to stock enough peanut butter and ice cream, although he has been known to run out of freeze-dried crickets.

As Guidance Counselor, Drake works with children who are scared of the animals. He uses many approaches, including counting to ten, deep breathing, and picturing the animals in their underwear.

As School Nurse, Robin gives out Band-Aids, cough drops, and ginger ale. But she doesn't need to use them very much. Mostly, she helps kids figure out what they really need to feel better.

As Admissions Director, Ursula is in charge of attracting more students to the school to more fully realize Zoolinda's dream. As Ms. Font likes to say, "Always put your best foot (or hoof or paw) forward." Ursula is the perfect person to assist in this area since she is an expert on how schools are *supposed* to look.

Ursula is also helping Ms. Font to learn to use a computer. Some people (but not Ms. Font) say, "You can't teach an old dog new tricks." Thankfully, this doesn't seem to be the case for elephants. Ms. Font has found that the end of her trunk is much better suited to typing e-mails than answering the phone or writing with pencils (no matter how large).

If you happen to see the newest issue of *Zooey!*, you will not be able to miss the newest ad, designed with Ursula's help and typed by Ms. Font herself:

Welcome to the Zoolinda Gray Academy!
✿ ✿ ✿

Formerly known as the Zoo School, the Zoolinda Gray Academy is a unique learning environment that values truth, imagination, and friendship. Here at ZGA our motto is "Let the Animals Be Your Textbooks!"

Kids, you will never have so much fun learning!

Parents, our rigorous academic program will provide your child with the basic skills he or she needs in school and, more importantly, in life.

We also offer the following special programs:

★ *Its Bark Is Worse Than Its Bite:* How to get over your fear of animals

★ *Pass the Peanut Butter, Please:* Why peanut butter is the perfect food for children and elephants

★ *Healthy as a Horse:* How to feel good without the use of Band-Aids

★ *Why Are Flamingos Pink?* 1,000 facts about animals you can really use in your daily life

★ *Not Everything Is Black and White:* How to see things as they really are

Super-Duper Top-Rated Gold Seal of Approval awarded this year by L.I.O.N.S. (Learned Inspectors of New Schools)

For more information,
visit us on the web at www.zoolindagrayacademy.com
or e-mail Ms. Ella Font, Principal
at EllaFont@zoolindagrayacademy.com

Ella Font's Book of Sayings

A new book filled with old wisdom from the beloved principal of the Zoo School.

"Everyone should read this book. It's more important than the dictionary!" —Ursula Wright, student

"I give this book three gold seals of approval!" —Inspector #3, L.I.O.N.S

The newest exhibit, "Australian Woodland Wonderland," is now open at the zoo! Located in the former Zoo School classroom, it features a variety of Australian marsupials, birds, and other animals in a forest of baby eucalyptus trees.

(continued from page 4)

A Study of the Effects of Sugar on Flamingos
by Kitty Katz

and so this study shows that while shrimp are excellent for giving flamingos their pink color, many other food substances work just as well, including cherry ices, watermelon, and strawberry ice cream. Foods with high sugar content have the added benefit of making flamingos more energetic, and likely to perform silly tricks, such as hopping up and down on one foot, whistling, and playing Ring Around the Rosy, behaviors seldom seen in flamingos.

REFLECTIONS ON A HIPPOPOTAMUS
by Gray N. Large

Everything you always wanted to know about hippos and many things you probably never wanted to know, all in one convenient 967-page volume. The experts say:

"This book is indispensable for anyone serious about studying the hippopotamus." —Ms. Hummingfly, Zookeeper

"I particularly recommend pages 37, 299, and 426."
—Mr. Dapple, Zookeeper